Ever Since

Ever Since

ALENA BRUZAS

Rocky Pond Books

ROCKY POND BOOKS
An imprint of Penguin Random House LLC, New York

First published in the United States of America by Rocky Pond Books,
an imprint of Penguin Random House LLC, 2023

Copyright © 2023 by Alena Bruzas

Rocky Pond Books & colophon are trademarks of Penguin Random House LLC.
The Penguin colophon is a registered trademark of Penguin Books Limited.

Visit us online at penguinrandomhouse.com.

Library of Congress Cataloging-in-Publication Data is available.

Printed in the United States of America
ISBN 9780593616178

10 9 8 7 6 5 4 3 2 1

BVG

Design by Cerise Steel
Text set in TT Tricks

CONTENT NOTE: Please be advised that this book contains depictions of sexual assault, CSA, and suicidal ideation.

To Anita Hill, for speaking truth to power.
To Chanel Miller, for letting us know your name.
To the people who spoke first, despite abuse and opposition,
so we could follow.
To all the girls.

One

ONCE THERE WERE five princesses. No, I mean five witches. Actually, they were goddesses. Anyway, whatever they were, they were friends.

Once there were five friends.

And the story goes like this:

It's finally summer and we're road-tripping out to the coast. Poppy is driving, so of course I'm sitting shotgun. Ramona, Paz, and Thalia take photos of their faces squished together. I say we have to make a pact to keep our phones in the glove box and we're singing to the radio until it dissolves into static and then we play the license plate game and now we're playing truth or dare. I tell Ramona to flash the SUV next to us and she gets me back by daring me to hang my butt out the window.

"Ro!" I squeal.

"Virginia!" she squeals back, and throws a scrunchie at me and says I have to do it and so I do and I think I'm going to die when Poppy goes around a corner and I almost fall out the window.

We get to La Push in time for sunset. The floor of the car is covered in garbage and my foot is asleep and our limbs are overlapping and intermingled. Thalia is braiding strands of

Poppy's hair and I'm painting Paz's toenails and Ro is eating the sandwich that Thalia packed for herself.

We tumble out of the car with our arms around each other, holding hands and bumping hips, and the bond of our friendship seems enduring, like nothing can break it, ever. But as Edison spots us and bellows my name and I feel Thalia's eyes all over my skin, I'm afraid it won't be enough.

We're camping on the beach. No one questions whether or not it's allowed. We just pitch our tents and lay out our sleeping bags and start drinking. The beach is crowded with bare feet and loose waves and fraying cutoff shorts. I change into my bathing suit but I don't go swimming. Nobody swims in the ocean here. It's too cold. Even in summer you don't go swimming off the coast of Washington.

Ro gets the fire going after Thalia relents and lets us use her Trader Joe's bags as kindling and the boys wander over all casual to drink our beer and eat our hot dogs. Rumi is putting his arm around Poppy's shoulders and kissing her neck and squeezing her thigh and she keeps leaning away and shrugging, but he isn't picking up on her don't-touch-me-I'm-going-to-puke signals. I can tell she's drunk because her breath smells sweet like maybe whiskey and her eyes are wide. Poppy always gets extra innocent, like, *Who, me?*

Rumi probably thinks it's no big deal because they're going out, but I can tell Poppy is annoyed and it doesn't help that she keeps taking shots. It's funny how a night can change like that. How it can feel so good to sit under the salty sprawling night sky with your toes in the sand that's still warm and the fire crackling and the sparks drifting and the ocean intoning nearby. Then suddenly you feel like you might puke and also people are probably possibly judging you right now because you're drunk and sloppy and getting groped.

Poppy covers her mouth and stumbles toward the rocks and Rumi follows her like he probably thinks a good boyfriend should. I follow too because I know what's coming.

"Just piss off!" Poppy says. I almost laugh because she sounds like a British gangster, but then she bends over and I hear a splatter. Rumi hovers, his hands in his pockets and looking at his feet.

"I've got it," I say to Rumi.

He looks uncertain. Poppy yells piss off again and Rumi blushes and glances at me and then he leaves and I feel sorry for him. Poppy grabs my arm and I stagger and scrape my heel on a rock. She throws up again, so I just grit my teeth and let her hold on to me and keep her hair out of her face.

When she's done I wrap my arm around her waist and she leans on me all the way back to our tent. I take off the rain flap because the sky is clear and the wind feels good. We lie down side by side, my fake blond mixed with her real black, and she takes my hand and threads her fingers through mine.

She's quiet for so long that I think she's asleep. When I start to get up she squeezes my hand tighter. "I love you," she says with her eyes still closed.

. . .

I find Rumi sitting alone, playing chicken with the tide. His feet are stretched out and wet from the waves. "She's just drunk," I say. "It's not about you. She always gets pissed when she's sick." My scraped heel is throbbing. He doesn't answer, so I examine my foot. It's still bleeding and there's sand in the cut.

"What happened?" he asks.

I shrug.

Rumi stands up. "Wait here." When he comes back he pulls my foot into his lap. It stings when he pours cold water over the scrape. As he applies Neosporin and a Band-Aid, I realize that I am so absolutely determined not to flirt with him that I have no idea what to say. I pull my leg back and wedge my bandaged foot under my butt.

By the fire Paz starts singing and Thalia is sitting in Edison's lap and Ro yells something at Edison about punching him in the face, which he probably deserves but I think Ro is joking. The party oozes out away from the fire, small circles of kids here and there, and Paz and Thalia and Ro run down and splash their ankles in the water, lithe and silver in the moonlight. Edison grabs a six-pack and walks off, leaning to the side like a dilapidated house.

I tell myself every time, this is the last time. Thalia is suspicious but she doesn't actually know. If I stop now maybe she'll never find out. But then Edison looks over his shoulder at me. I stand up, straightening my bikini bottom and brushing sand off my butt. I feel Rumi watching as I follow Edison but I don't look back. There are enough people here now that no one will notice, I don't think.

The moon is almost full and it shivers across the water and for a minute I feel beautiful in the bending light. So I kiss him and of course we . . .

(I can't even say it.)

I can still hear the singing, the cackling laughter, the lewd jokes of the party.

I come home to Poppy like I always come home to her. Whether it's her house or the lunch table at school or here in the tent. I watch her breathe, in and out, in and out. It seems so easy for her.

Nobody was up when I got back from Edison. The fire was almost dead. Just a few embers glowing in the ash. I watched it for a while and drank from a bottle of red wine that somebody left open and halfway buried in the sand.

Now I lie with the bottle cradled in the crook of my arm and when it's empty I fall asleep on my wine-stained pillow and bad dreams lap at my neck but I won't remember them in the morning.

Before we leave, Ramona says we have to swim. "It's the summer before senior year. It will never be like this again."

"We have next summer, Rowie." Paz crosses her arms and squints away.

"Next summer we won't be in high school anymore, Paz," Ro says. "We'll all be off doing our own things. I'm going to France and Thalia wants to start early at school and your mom wants to visit your family in Brazil."

Thalia smiles with the sun on her face and leans back in the sand, closing her eyes. Poppy glowers into her coffee and I say, "What about me, Ro? Where will I be?"

Ro gives me a look that is wistful and uncertain. "You'll be sweeping cobwebs from the sky, Virginia. But you'll be with us by and by."

My toes are buried in sea foam. Ro puts her brown foot on top of my pale one. Her toenails are red and mine are teal. Our feet look nice like that, side by side and overlapping. She tucks a lock of hair behind my ear and I smile at her freckles, which I love. She's reassuring me in her own way, I know. Maybe she's not sure where I'll end up, but she has faith in me to figure it out, is what she's saying.

"So are we doing this?" Poppy's hungover and pissed about it.

"Fine," Paz says, but then she smiles and reaches for Thalia.

We run into the water holding hands. A wave rushes up to meet us like frozen blue static. We scream and Poppy squeezes my hand so hard it hurts. And then I am submerged, immersed, surrounded by cold so shocking, I can't breathe or think. And for a second I feel terrified and almost lost like I'll be swept out to that infinite blue sea. But to the right and left of me I am anchored to these girls. With them, I am safe.

Two

ON THE WAY home Thalia and Paz ride with Edison. Ro sprawls out in the back and falls asleep with her feet hanging out the window. Poppy loads a bowl. She's still hungover and now she's carsick, so I'm driving even though it's her car.

"Soccer is starting this week," she says.

"Are you dreading it?" I ask. I can't imagine why anybody would actually want to spend time with a bunch of eleven-year-olds.

"I like the kids. They're hilarious."

I smile at the road. It's so Poppy. To her, it's not even a good deed.

"Me and Edison, you know, again," I say.

"Was it good?" Poppy refuses to judge me.

"Yeah, mostly."

"What were the bad parts?"

"He's a sloppy kisser. He got spit all over my face and shoved his tongue way too far down my throat. I almost gagged."

Poppy laughs, covering her eyes. We come up on a curve and, reckless, I speed up, screeching as we tilt and the woods and the ocean rush by in blurs of green and blue and my entire world seems precarious. Poppy whoops and sails her hand out the window.

"You know, it's fine. It's just that I don't think you like doing it," Poppy says after a while.

"It's fine? You really think it's fine what I'm doing?" I glance back at Ro. She's still asleep.

Poppy leans back and closes her eyes. "I mean, like, in a cosmic sense. We're seventeen. It's not like Thalia and Edison are married with kids. I mean, like, it's all just drama. There's no major consequences."

"You mean, like, you mean, like."

She laughs. "Piss off."

The thing is with Poppy, there's no hiding. She looks at me and I look back at her. "But I feel bad about it," I say.

"Then why do you do it?"

She's hogging the weed. I grab it and take a hit. "Puff puff pass yo," I say with my mouth full of smoke.

"Virginia," Poppy says. "Why do you do it?"

"I convince myself I want it, in the moment."

"And then after?"

"Like last night after Edison and I hooked up, I felt like a pot that had been scoured." I take another hit and hand the pipe back to Poppy. "That's a weird way to put it."

"I get it. Empty."

"And like scraped out."

"You should stop."

"Stop what though?"

"Stop doing things that make you feel bad," Poppy says.

"But there are so many things that make me feel bad and I never know which it will be. And I have you. And you always make me feel better." I give her a shitty smile like I know I'm an asshole and I know she loves me anyway.

We pull into the line for the ferry. In the back seat Ro grunts and sits up, wiping drool from her mouth. "I smell pot," she says.

Poppy drives through downtown Seattle traffic, after the ferry docks. It smells like salt and seaweed and cold wind and then it smells like exhaust and hot pavement. She grunts in frustration every time she changes gears in her hand-me-down muscle car. Ro scrolls through songs on her phone, searching for the perfect one.

I wish we had camped an extra night. Or I wish we had stopped and stayed in some tiny coastal town, some run-down bed-and-breakfast on a run-down road with clapboard houses and American flags snapping in the wind. But we didn't. We're here.

We park and Ro runs to her house and her mom comes out, down the stairs. We were only gone for two days, but they walk with their arms around each other's waists, talking like it's been months and they have so much to catch up on.

My house, across the curve from Poppy's, is dark and the shades are drawn, but I can hear the music pounding through the door.

"I think Mom is making pizza on the grill tonight," Poppy says, as if she assumes I'm spending the night. As if Willow, Poppy's mom, will assume I'm spending the night.

I can smell the orange blossoms from the tree in the yard

between Poppy's house and mine as we slip past. Since that first night at Poppy's when we were almost twelve, I haven't slept in my closet or crouched behind the oak tree in the backyard. I haven't tried to get invited to some friend's house only to be told no because it's a school night. Willow always lets me.

Inside her house, everything seems so normal. It's clean and there's food in the fridge and Willow is sitting on the deck drinking iced tea. She asks us about the trip and she says I need some aloe for my sunburn and then she starts the grill and I close my eyes and listen. To the conversation, to the birds, to the wind in the treetops, to the *tap tap tap* of cutting tomatoes and onions and peppers.

I think about that first night. About the keen relief of not being home when He was there. Of not having to avoid Him or to feel the compulsion to smile at Him and then the discomfort of actually smiling. About how Poppy lent me her best pair of pajamas and gave me her best pillow to sleep on as if it were no big deal. As if it were just a normal night.

"Virginia," Willow says.

I open my eyes and look at her, smiling and normal.

"Do you want some?" she asks, holding up a pitcher of ice cubes and lemons and tea.

And I pretend to be normal too, like I always do, like I have been, ever since.

So I have this book. It's big and heavy and full of sun and sky colors. It's called *D'Aulaires' Book of Greek Myths*. My fourth-grade teacher gave it to me. She had to be kind of sneaky about it because it was a pretty obvious display of favoritism, but that was the year I showed up to school with handprint-shaped bruises on my shoulders.

I spent the year reading and rereading the book in a shady spot of the reservoir park. When it was raining or getting dark, a lot of times I would go to Thalia's house. And her door was always open, figuratively and literally. Their doors and windows are open all year, almost. The rain comes misting in, and the air and the wind and the sun.

Thalia wasn't as obsessed with the book as I was, but she liked the story of Daphne. My favorite was always Medea. We would have these really intense discussions about Hades versus Hel versus Lucifer and the evolution of mythology and religion.

Poppy is sleeping next to me and I'm staring at the ceiling. Next year I'm taking the Comparative History of Ideas class, and the teacher requires a senior project. I keep thinking about doing it on folklore. Mythology and fairy tales. Once upon a time. Once upon a time there was a little girl. Once upon a time there was a beautiful princess. And she lived happily ever after.

I slide my phone out from under the pillow. *Hey,* I text Thalia.

What's up? she responds. *How's Poppy?*

asleep and cranky

How can you be asleep and cranky at the same time?

shes hungover enough to manage i promise, I text.

Thalia texts me a GIF of a panda falling over, which is supposed to be Poppy, I think.

so i was thinking about doing my senior project on folklore, I text her.

Like what about? Thalia replies.

not sure yet, maybe mythology? like daphne or something

That sounds cool.

right, do you want to partner up?

It takes Thalia so long to respond, I start to get paranoid.

Okay, she says.

I stare at the word until my eyes hurt from the glare. She said okay. Maybe now I can fix it. Fix what Edison broke.

I send her a bunch of hearts and roll over, smiling into my pillow.

Thalia always thought there was a definite difference between fairy tales and mythology. Fairy tales are different from mythology is different from religion. Fairy tales are like Disney movies. Sleeping Beauty, Snow White, Cinderella. Something that the Brothers Grimm probably wrote or maybe Hans Christian Andersen. A princess gets saved from an evil witch by a handsome prince and they lived happily ever after the end forever and ever.

Mythology is like Zeus, you know? Or maybe Odin Allfather and super-hot Thor, but that's in the Marvel movies. And that's where I think she's wrong. It all bleeds together. Thor used to be somebody's god, somebody's religion. Then he became a myth and now he's a hot Australian actor who's actually an alien who speaks Shakespearean English. None of it makes sense. All of it, mythology, religion, fairy tales, all it is, all it ever has been, is the stories we tell. The stories we tell to make sense of things.

In the dark when you're scared, the thunder is booming and the world is shaking and everything might come down around you and there's a beast, a monster, a wolf coming to get you. When things feel beyond your control. You tell yourself a story.

Once upon a time.

I wake up before Poppy. I sleep so well here, I always wake up first. I slip out of bed and downstairs to the den where we have our sleepovers when it's all of us. The couch that Thalia and Paz always claim, their feet crossing and overlapping in the corner of the sectional. The chaise where Ro sleeps, lounging like a princess in a Renaissance painting. And me and Poppy make a nest on the floor, blankets and couch cushions and these long floor pillows that we found at Target covered in peacocks and paisley prints and dahlias. I sleep better when I'm next to Poppy.

The morning light is blue and diffuse and the dew sparkles like Cinderella's dress, tiny lights on leaves and flowers. When I manage to wake up for it, this is my favorite time of day. I drink some of Willow's mint tea and wait for Poppy. She comes creeping down, tired but not grouchy, rubbing dreams out of her eyes. I hand her my tea, hot through the mug in the morning cold air, and she takes a drink.

"Let's go for a run," she says eventually.

"I don't want to."

"Come on, it will feel good. You'll be glad when we get out there."

We sync up our music and start out fast, racing like we always do, and we're pushing past our seven-minute mile. I can feel the seconds falling behind me, slipping away in our slipstream, until we're sprinting. Poppy throws her arms up and yells along with her favorite line of the song and I put my hands up in the air when the song tells me to and she does a move like a lawn mower, pretending to be a dad-dancer, and the sun is in our eyes and the air is perfect warm.

It rained last night and there are puddles in the dips and cracks of the sidewalk. I jog in place as Poppy stoops to rescue a fat earthworm stretching, reaching for dirt and flowers. She always does this. Not just for worms—for any bug, even spiders. Thalia calls her the steward of small things.

My feet are wet with puddle water and I want to shower and put on clean clothes and my house is quiet now. "I'll come over later," I say.

"I have that soccer coach orientation thing," she says. "I'll text you when I'm back."

We never say goodbye. Somehow she knows I need to know that she'll always be there. It's never goodbye. There's always later.

"Okay," I say.

"Love you," she says.

"You," I say.

"No, you."

And I wave her off into the sunlight.

We all grew up here in this cul-de-sac. Paz and Thalia share a fence at the back of the curve under a tall ponderosa that kills the grass and smells like pine sap and dust in the summer. Ro lives on the corner closest to the rest of the world. Where you can hear the noise from Fifteenth two streets over. Where the bus stops just behind Pagliacci's that makes the pesto primavera we used to celebrate birthdays with, feeling like we were fancy.

The reservoir park is behind my fence, dark and safe and cold or lovely warm or mostly something in between. In seventh grade we climbed over my fence and smoked weed in the park for the first time. Ro got paranoid and Paz got loud and I stared at the underside of the leaves of the birch tree, silver bells in the wind. In ninth grade Ro dared me to streak and then changed it to just moon them from the sidewalk but I didn't hear that part and ran naked through the park dodging yellow streetlights, cold and kind of thrilled. I got dressed behind them, hiding in the shadows of the fence, while Ro and Poppy and Thalia and Paz were bent over with laughter because I streaked naked even though that wasn't actually the dare.

At first I didn't know them. I watched from my front stoop. Ro with her parents who actually paid attention to her, taking her on walks or loading her into her booster seat going who-knows-where. Thalia and Paz at the other end of the street, small faraway forms drawing giant chalk trees in front of their houses or Hula-Hooping or cartwheeling or trying to ride their bikes with no hands. Even after me and Thalia became friends in third grade, I felt like an outsider. Then Poppy moved in, an unclaimed girl, who maybe could be all mine.

Poppy gathered us. When she moved here we gathered around her. She invited us all over and we all came and then we were a group. We weren't before, but when Poppy came we formed. And then her home became my home, more than my own.

The houses in our neighborhood, Thalia's house, Paz's house, Ro's house, they're Sears Craftsman. I looked it up once because I like them so much and they're so different than my house. Mine is a big ugly split-level we bought from an old lady and it still smells like old lady even though it's been years. The toilet is stained and the cupboard doors are warped.

The debris from the party my dad must have had last night is scattered over the carpet in the living room, trailing through the kitchen and the dining room into the bathroom. There is a small splatter of puke on the linoleum next to the toilet. The kitchen counters are littered with empty bottles and scarlet rings of wine. The garbage can is out from under the sink and stuffed with pizza boxes and crumpled bags of chips. I take the pizza boxes out and set them on the counter to put them in the compost later.

There's a beer bottle filled with cigarette butts on my nightstand. The air smells stale and rank. Somebody probably passed out in my bed last night.

I rip off the sheets and open the window and lock the door and lie down on a spare blanket from the hall closet. I cover my head with my uncased pillow and fall asleep.

*O*nce upon a time there was this beautiful princess who was also a goddess who was also a witch. Her name was Medea. (I know you've heard of her.)

She lived in a faraway land far away from everything everything even the gods where the sands were black and hot and the water was gray and it churned with monsters and in the forest of conifers beyond her kingdom there lurked creeping creatures and crawling creatures that scared and fascinated Medea and sometimes she crept there with them learning their secrets and their spells.

She was the granddaughter of Helios the god of the sun (before Apollo, that usurper). She didn't like the gods. She didn't like heroes either. She heard of Jason before he came. She heard of his bold quest, him and his Argonauts, to claim her golden fleece. But it was guarded by the never-sleeping dragon to whom Medea fed fresh apricots that dripped like honey juices and whom Medea petted and whom Medea loved.

She heard of Jason and she knew he could never take the fleece from her never-sleeping dragon. She heard of him and she knew he would fail, but then she saw him and there was just something something something about him. Medea fell in love with him. Fell hard. (It was like magic.)

In the end she helped him steal the fleece, she helped him thwart her father, she helped him kill her dragon, she helped him escape her kingdom, and she loved him so much so much that she went with him. And they lived happily ever after. (Right?)

Three

I WAKE UP to my mom yelling fuck you, presumably to my dad. The garage door opens and the floor vibrates beneath my bed. The bass from his subwoofers is so loud and low that I feel my skull waver to it, kowtowing, submitting. It's too strong and all my bones know it. It's like an assault. Everything my dad does is like an assault.

As the look-at-me noise fades I hear something so familiar, it would be comforting if it weren't so terribly sad. My mom crying.

I almost ignore it and go back to sleep.

Just like I always almost ignore it.

I've spent years trying to ignore it.

I am so sick of it. But.

She's in the bathroom with the water running (as if that covers anything up). I sit on my mom's bed and wait. She comes out, her face washed and cold-creamed and shiny and not quite new, and she tugs her sleeve down over her red and raw wrist and I avert my eyes just like we've agreed in not so many words.

"Hi honey," she says. "Want to watch *Friends*?"

I rest my head on her shoulder just the way I know she likes. I let the bright palette of *Friends* blur into a bleeding watercolor and let her sniffles be muffled by the laughing live studio audience.

She falls asleep quickly. I guess she took something. Or several somethings. The clock on the nightstand says it's only eight. I need to get out of here.

I lean into Ro's dresser and take a picture of her doing her lips. I knock her perfume over with my butt and Thalia laughs and I spray my wrists. "Mmm, what is this?"

"J'adore." Ro affects a French accent.

"Ugh, I have the worse zit," Thalia says.

"Want me to pop it?" Paz says, sticking her face in Thalia's and looking at her skin.

"Get away, you sicko," Thalia yells.

"Seriously, ugh!" I say, shuddering.

"It's satisfying," Paz says.

"Can I use your concealer?" Thalia says.

"Doi, I only have my skin color, colonizer," Ro says, and crosses her eyes at Thalia.

Paz shrugs and I dig around in my bag until I find an almost empty tube and hand it to Thalia. I check my phone again for a text from Poppy. "I'm sick of Isaiah and his dumb friends," I say, and of course I mean Edison. I glance at Thalia but she's ignoring me now, staring at the mirror, dabbing at her chin.

"But Isaiah has the best house and he's having people over tonight, so shut yo mouth, woman," Paz says, and I take a picture of her sticking her tongue out at me.

"Where's Poppy?" Thalia says.

Everybody looks at me. I hold up my empty phone and shrug. "Where indeed?" I say.

"You haven't heard from her?" Paz says.

"I've texted her like twenty times. We were supposed to hang out this afternoon but, like, nothing."

It's a weird silence. A strange empty moment that feels airless. For so long we've gathered around Poppy. They all keep looking at me like I should know where she is, but she's not texting me back. I shrug again.

Ro stands up and spins, her braids flaring out and her skirt skimming her butt. "How much of a hooch do I look like?" she says. She makes a kissy face, her lips purple and glowing against her chestnut skin.

"Just the right amount of hooch," says Thalia. She's wearing a sprigged romper. I like it better than my sundress. She sees me eyeing her. "What?"

I swirl my skirt a little. "This would look so good on you!"

"I'm not wearing the right bra for it," she says.

"We can trade! Come on, we're the exact same size and it will look better on you than it does on me."

She narrows her eyes at me. "We're not eleven anymore, Virginia."

When we used to trade clothes and pretend to be twins. Back when our friendship came easier. When I didn't have to fight for every smile.

"Fine! I was just trying to do you a favor."

Paz rolls her eyes from the bed, but I know she's not judging.

We're allowed to care. We're allowed to look good and be excited that we look good and being excited doesn't mean we're shallow. We all have nice even features and skill with makeup and just the right clothes, which sometimes means trading when Thalia isn't being a hooch. Paz is the real beauty, Brazilian and Indigenous Hawaiian, with flawless golden skin and long black hair and brown eyes like crushed velvet but she plays it down. If she wears makeup she looks airbrushed perfect and people stare. I pretend I don't but I notice people looking at us when we're all together. All together, all combined, we add up to something more than the sum of our parts and something split into equal parts.

We are part jealous, part lascivious, part in love.

In the dark and silence we slip by lit-up houses, like glowing Norman Rockwell paintings. We duck beneath my window, Poppy's, Thalia's, Paz's, giggling, feeling stealthy, feeling devious, feeling excited.

But we're ready to be loud and we run through the narrow dark reservoir park, holding hands, shrieking, ready. The music is pounding when we get to Isaiah's and it floods through my body like it's electric. I grab Thalia and Ro, and Paz starts screaming the lyrics, and we jump up and down to the beat like maniacs, and I feel like I am insane and I don't even care about all the things everybody is saying about me.

But of course it doesn't last, because Edison starts slinking through the room. He touches my hip and he stands between me and Thalia and she shrieks and throws her arms around his neck. Her cheeks are flushed and her eyes are bright like she feels amazing, like this is the best moment of her life. Because Edison is her boyfriend and he's gorgeous and he smells just right and they're dancing. But she doesn't know that now he's reaching back. He's touching my arm, my thigh, my bare skin, trying to entwine me. Like he thinks we're all going to tumble into bed together and he's finally going to get that threesome he's been dreaming about.

And I'm almost lured into his fantasy, I'm ashamed to admit. But then the song changes and Langston bumps into me and smiles an apology and at the same time his hand closes around Paz's shoulder oh-so-carefully. But it's too late.

Thalia noticed. She saw the one second that I touched Edison back and that's all it takes. Her face slams shut like a door and she turns. She looks away. She leaves.

And I'm left spinning in the darkness.

Maybe it's just awkward. Maybe nobody noticed after all. Thalia disappeared and then I couldn't find Paz or Ro. I go outside looking for them and the party has spilled out into the yard anyway.

I take a long drink from the bottle of gin that I brought from home. It's gross, but it was full. Thalia and Edison are across from me. He's waving around a whole bottle of champagne he probably stole from Isaiah's parents like he's so fucking cool. Thalia snatches it and takes a massive drink, wiping her chin and laughing into Edison's face, being charming and beautiful and fun and free. Is she faking? Does he really make her happy? I wonder if this confirmed it for her, about him and me.

I drink some more disgusting gin wishing it were delicious champagne and I don't care that I probably look like a creeper over here with my bottle and my scowl and maybe I should just go home. But it doesn't take him long. It never does. I don't, I don't, I don't understand his thing with me. I'm not even, like, better looking than Thalia. I mean, we're practically twins. Maybe that's it. Maybe he's into twins. Sicko. Pervert. He digs his fingers into my arm and pulls me along while I try to find the gin bottle with my mouth. I giggle into the bubbly echoes and then choke down a mouthful.

"What are you laughing about?" Edison asks. He leans against the side of Isaiah's house. The party noise is not so distant, but distant enough, I guess.

"Just I'm a slut and it's funny, you know," I say.

"I do know," he says, and lights his blunt. He reaches for me.

"Edison."

"What?"

"I just." I can't think of what to say. I can't think of how to leave without offending him or hurting his feelings or making things awkward. I lean my head back against the wall and close my eyes to the stars that are low and lush tonight. He's touching me. His hands are underneath my dress, pushing it to the

side. Beneath my bra. I take a hit from the blunt and I am floating up and up and up like I am a balloon, a red balloon, all my
color and all my red dwindling in the dark, fading, fading.

"Hey," somebody says through my eyelids.

It's Rumi.

"What's up?" Edison says. After a pause he removes his
hands from under my dress.

Rumi smiles at me, but there's a crease between his eyebrows. I drink him in. His long body leaning back like the air
supports his weight. His dark brown hair with a slight wave, long
enough to tuck behind his ear. There's a hole in his earlobe, a
vacant piercing. His skin, warmer and deeper russet because of
the summer sun. Each detail stands out and also how he looks
at me like maybe he cares about what happens next. Like it matters to him if Edison leaves me alone or not. Even if I'm trying to
pretend it doesn't matter to me.

I offer the blunt to Rumi. "Thanks," he says with his mouth
full of smoke. "So, like, have you heard from Poppy?"

Edison looks away, at the dark nothing behind the trees.

"No, not all day. Have you? I don't know where she is." I put
space between me and Edison and I feel it when he notices and
steps closer to me again. He isn't ready to give up yet, and I
don't think he cares what Rumi thinks.

And then Rumi closes in as well. They study each other. For
a second all pretenses are gone. Then Edison shakes his head
and sucks on his blunt and blows smoke up into the dark air.
And I feel it, the exact second he's done caring. He laughs like

he's incredulous, like I'm acting crazy, like he's above my stupid drama. And so I slink around the side of the house and Rumi follows me.

We sit against the fence. I pull my legs close and wrap my arms around my knees and hold myself so tight, I stop shaking. I can't think of what to say.

I take a drink of gin but I don't offer any to Rumi. It's mine anyway.

I think it's possible people are talking about me right now.

Maybe about me and Rumi.

About what a slut I am.

About how I'll fuck anyone.

About how even as soon as Poppy's not around I start fucking with Rumi.

I stand up and I feel like I have eyes all over my skin like my skin is too tight for my body like I want to peel it off and step out of myself and be somebody else. Rumi touches my wrist and I feel like the stares intensify and I turn and leave. I find the sidewalk, stumble down down down the hill, watch my feet, twist my ankle. Then Rumi's hand is on my arm just above my elbow, guiding my faltering feet.

"Virginia," Rumi says, and his hand is warm. "Let's sit down for a minute."

Ravenna Park is halfway here and halfway there. Up from the ravine and the creek there is a little playground. I find the swings. I find my feet and I watch them, dragging through the gravel that's all dim and gray in the night.

Rumi says, "Maybe you should go home."

I sway on the swings. "I don't want to go home."

"Okay," Rumi says, and he kicks his feet back and starts to swing. "Let's race."

The wind is cold and it rushes by my face and flings my hair back and the skirt of my dress against my thighs and we laugh so hard as we race to be the highest swing, to kick a hole in the sky, we laugh so hard that I feel like I can't breathe.

"Childhood is not over yet," Rumi says, slowing down.

My heart is pounding and my head is clear. I hear a frog gurgle somewhere nearby and I am just enough drunk and just enough not to have a visceral memory of soft wet frog skin in my hand, struggling against my palm, tickling, making me giggle. Even here, in this very park, I used to catch them. I perk like I am a cat and I smell a mouse.

"What?" Rumi says.

"A frog," I say. There it is again, down the hill. I follow it with Rumi laughing behind me. "Can you hear it? It's close," I say. I take my shoes off, set them on a rock. My feet are in the mud and my ankles are wet, splashed with creek water.

Rumi crouches next to me. "There," he says, pointing.

I creep closer, closer. I see it. A little hunched shadow. Rumi grins at me. His eyes gleam. I lunge forward and I do, I touch it, but as soon as I feel the slick wet muscles straining against my hand I scream and fall back, ass in the water. My dress is wet and I can't stop laughing. The frog belches in protest and hops to another rock. Then it freezes again like of course we can't see it now that it's moved a little.

Rumi is bent over, breathless with laughter.

"I used to be so good at catching frogs," I say.

Rumi sits in the mud next to me and puts his arm around my shoulders, still laughing. He pulls me in tight and then releases me. "I can still see it," he says. He scoots forward and pulls his sleeve up around his forearm, white cotton glowing against his skin. For a moment everything is still, frozen, even the trees stop rustling in the wind. Rumi's hand strikes out like a snake and the frog disappears beneath his knuckles. I shriek and put my hands over my mouth.

"Here," he says, and drops the frog in my lap.

Quick before it hops away I grab it. The frog pokes its head between my fingers and I hold it up, peering into its eyes. "Hello," I say.

It hops away and we catch it again. And again and again. Poor little frog. But I love it. All of it. The cool night. The creek. The trees above us. The stars that are dim behind all the street-lights and houselights and headlights. I love Rumi warm beside me. I love the hum of nighttime insects singing to the moon. But most of all I love my wet skin, my muddy dress, my messy face, my tangled hair. I love this version of myself.

I point with the frog in my hand. "Under those rocks over there in the summer there are like a million garter snakes. I used to catch them and tuck them into my shirt and keep them there and they would wiggle around and then get sleepy against my body heat."

"Oh my god." Rumi laughs. "Give me the frog," he says.

I give the frog a kiss and hand it over.

"I think it's time to release the little guy," Rumi says. He holds the frog up to the water. "Goodbye, little friend," he says. "Be free."

The frog sits in Rumi's open hand and then hops into the creek and disappears under the sheen of moonlight on the black water.

Rumi is looking at me. He is looking at me like I am something beautiful and he is drinking me in. I close my eyes and let the night wash over me.

The thing is, before Poppy and Rumi, before Edison and me, there was a minute when I thought it would be Rumi and me. It was the first two weeks of last summer. Poppy was at an arts camp and then she was training to be a lifeguard at the public pool and Ro was on that big trip with her mom and Paz was in Brazil and Thalia was just starting to date Edison. So nobody was ever around and I was bored and I ran the track at the community center training for who-knows-what but also just because it felt so good to push and push and push my body. And Rumi was there playing basketball.

I'm good at basketball. I don't even like watching it, but it's like when I'm running. I stop thinking. I sink into the burn and stretch and sweat and suddenly I'm doing it and I'm good at it. I'd play with Rumi and he was right there, next to me, close to me, touching me, and I could smell him and feel his heat and it was there. That shallow breathing, that quick heartbeat, that smile we're both trying to repress. It was there, I felt it.

And then once we almost kissed. He walked me home and it

was dark and we stopped at the reservoir park and he spun me around so fast on the merry-go-round that when I got off I was dizzy and stumbled accidentally-on-purpose and he caught me and I played like I was fainting and he crashed onto the grass still holding me and I ended up in his lap and he wrapped his arms around me and I stayed there. And we stared at each other. And I was smiling and so was he and then he stopped smiling and he was just looking at my eyes and then at my lips and I knew it was going to happen but then it just didn't.

But I kept thinking it would.

But then somehow it didn't.

And then Poppy texted me, *omg guesswhatguesswhat.*

And I had no idea.

Four

I STAY UP way too late reading the *Ramayana*. I'm trying to distract myself. But I throw the book on the floor and it crackles like an old gum wrapper. I shouldn't treat it that way, I know. It's Poppy's and her grandpa's before that and I'm pretty sure he brought it from India when he immigrated here. But it's almost one in the morning and I can't get stupid Rumi out of my stupid head.

I creep down the hall. Even though I know it's a bad idea, I fall asleep on the couch watching Netflix.

The sound of a phone ringing wakes me up. It rings and rings and rings until it feels like an electric drill boring into my brain.

My dad was still out when I fell asleep but now he's sprawled on his ripped corduroy recliner in his underwear nursing a tall glass of something iced and black and probably full of Sailor Jerry. A horror movie is glowing green on his pallid face. The TV phone is ringing loud and there is a pale girl staring at it, her eyes like black holes. I close my eyes because I know something bad is going to happen and I don't want to see it.

The TV starts screaming and I burrow deeper into my blankets.

"Will you turn that down?" I hear my mom whisper. I guess

her multitude of pills wore off. I guess their fight wore off. I keep my eyes closed and I wonder what time it is.

"Stop," she says. "No, just turn it down."

My dad doesn't say anything.

"Virginia is right there."

"She's asleep." He's drunk. He doesn't slur but his voice always lilts up. Like he's so good-natured, like everything is amusing, like he's so easygoing, like everybody is his best friend. Until he doesn't get what he wants.

"Stop," she says again, quieter this time like she's already giving in.

I imagine my dad trying to pull her into the chair with him, touching her, grabbing her, wrapping his arms and hands around her wrists, her thighs, her waist, like tentacles. I imagine my mom resisting, pulling away, trying to smile, trying to laugh, it's no big deal, she's just tired, just let her go.

"She's fucking asleep." He's loud now, as if I'll sleep through anything.

"Let's go to bed." She has to appease him now because he's getting pissed.

"Fuck," he says.

I keep my breathing even.

"Come on baby, just come to bed."

"Just fuck off."

I don't squeeze my eyes shut because that is too obvious. I keep my face slack, relaxed, still.

"No, come on." She's pleading with him now.

Just go to bed. Just go to bed. Just go to bed.

"Just shut the fuck up and fuck off, Sharon. I don't even know why you're still fucking standing there. Just go the fuck to bed."

I try to just listen to the movie, the screaming and the ripping and the shallow frightened breathing because I know what's going to happen now, I know what my mom is going to do, what my dad manipulated her into doing, what she didn't want to do because I'm right here, but she could only resist for so long, and now I can't move because then they would know I've been awake the whole time, and so I just lie there and try to listen only to the movie, and not to my dad lying back in his chair, and not to my mom trying to make it quick and quiet, but there's a little bit of slurping and sliding and sighing, and eventually there's my dad grunting and my mom coughing, and then quiet footsteps, and then unobtrusive snoring, and then just the screaming and the ripping and the frightened shallow breathing.

The doors slam separately, one, then the other. Front door, garage door. My dad's bass makes its standard goodbye. My mom screeches away in her Jeep she thinks makes her look cool.

My arm hangs off the edge of the couch, long and pale, and my blue veins drip toward my wrist like wet watercolor. The light coming in from the north-facing windows is thin and washed out and in it I am less visible.

I feel like a ghost. Like maybe I don't actually exist. Everything is quiet and white. I sit up and look out the window. There are shadows moving around in the windows of Poppy's house behind the dogwood trees.

But when I text her there's no response.

Edison texts me and I delete it.

I text Thalia: *did poppy show up?*

In summer we always did the same thing. Poppy lifeguarded at the pool and the rest of us sat around and got tan (me and Thalia) and freckled (Ro) and more golden and lovely (Paz) and waited for Poppy to be done. Ever since she was old enough, two years ago. Before that we'd just hang around the pool and swim.

But Poppy always took the first steps, the first one to do the grown-up thing. She was the first to sign up for driver's ed and then get her license while the rest of us just took buses around or walked. She was the first one to get a job, babysitting the summer she was fourteen, all summer, five days a week, for two bratty kids who lived down the road from us. Then she lifeguarded when we were fifteen.

One by one the rest of us followed—reluctantly, but we did. Learning to drive, getting a job. We didn't until she led the way. When she led, we walked behind her.

But this year she signed up to coach soccer, a team of middle schoolers, leaving us to our own devices at the pool.

Thalia texts back: *Dad says no, she didn't. He's stuck coaching her team until he can find a replacement. And apparently Rumi's sister is there even. I guess she was really excited to be on Poppy's team. But she's not there.*

Edison texts me again.

My phone is hot in my hand.

She's not there.

But I don't have time to think about it anymore because I'm meeting Thalia to work on our senior project. So I just shower and dry off and put on lotion and makeup and blow-dry the ends of my hair and get dressed and try really really hard not to think about anything but stories and fairy tales and folklore and myth.

I knew it was a bad idea.

We're meeting at The Pearl, on The Ave. I'm late, so I take the bus even though it's close enough to walk. I dodge a group of kids sitting on the sidewalk outside the door. One of them, with blue hair and a plaid scarf even though it's hot out, goes to Elderberry, our school. Thalia waves to me through the painted window.

There is something in the emptiness that comes after sex. I can feel my walls that are scraped out and thin and close to breaking. And the aching nothingness within. That is the most of what I feel. The walls and the nothing.

Thalia is reading the weekly free newspaper, fingers on the page, totally engrossed.

"Have you heard of being turned on by sucking on some-body's nose? Apparently it's a thing. It's called nasolingus."

"Urgh," I say. Thalia closes the newspaper.

I knew it wasn't going to help anything.

"So what do you think?" I say. "I mean, we know we like Daphne. Should it be about her story?"

"That might not be enough material for, like, a whole year-long project."

I knew it was going to make everything worse but I wanted to feel skin on my skin and bones on my bones and heat in my cold cold body. Edison kept texting. And I kept texting Poppy and she kept not texting back. So I told Edison to come over. And he did. And we . . . And then he left. And now I'm here.

I resist rubbing my hands all over my face and smearing my eyeliner. Before Poppy moved here, for a little while Thalia was my best friend. Around when we were eleven. It was always her house I would go to. And her dad was always glad to see me. But then in middle school I started drinking. I started smoking pot and sometimes I did other stuff too. Ecstasy or shrooms or acid. I started making out and giving hand jobs and then giving blow jobs and then having sex. And that scared Thalia, I think—not that she didn't do all the same things eventually, but not until high school.

Me and Thalia never stopped being friends either, but our dynamic changed. She spent more time with Paz and Ro and I spent more time with whatever guy I was hooking up with at the moment. But then everybody started having sex and it wasn't a big deal anymore but the distance remained between us. And it still does. And I still miss her.

And then Edison and her started dating at the end of

sophomore year. It was like they were really in love. I hated it. It drove me crazy. It disgusted me. Thalia was stupid and romantic and naive. And Edison would definitely cheat on her.

She looks at me now. "Has there ever been a story that really resonated with you? Since the first time you heard it?"

I think of Edison, his face above me, not even seeing me.

"Medea," I say. "The story of Medea has always haunted me."

"Why do you think these stories have so much power? They've been around for thousands of years and people keep telling them," she says.

"Should that be where we start from? The power of stories?" I say.

"Why do they have so much power?" Thalia says.

"And the power of how they're told," I say. "How they're told, the telling of them, who's telling them, that also has power." I take the last drink of my coffee and when I look up, Thalia is looking past me, a friendly smile on her face. I turn and look over my shoulder. It's Rumi.

"Hey!" Thalia says. "You work here? How did we not know that?"

Rumi pours more coffee into my mug. It splashes a little and I cover it with my napkin. "It pays the bills," he says. "What are you all up to?"

"Senior project," Thalia says.

"You guys are already working on it?" Rumi says. He looks at me and I don't say anything and then back to Thalia.

She looks at me too. Then she says to Rumi, "Yeah, the teacher is really tough. But she has connections to the university and if we do a good job on the project, it can help, so me and Virginia are being proactive." She laughs and shrugs a little, like she's embarrassed by our ambition.

"What's it going to be about?" he says.

"We're not sure exactly. We're thinking the power of mythology? How come it stays around so long? I like the story of Daphne and Virginia likes Medea, so maybe Greek mythology?"

"That sounds interesting," he says.

They both look at me but again I don't say anything.

"Well, I'm almost off. I'll be back," Rumi says.

Thalia gives me a look. "Why are you being weird?"

"I, uh," I say, and then stop.

Thalia stares at me for a minute, her eyebrows low over her eyes. (How does she get her eyebrows so perfect? They're like straight out of the eighties.) "Okay, so, the power of mythology? Or the power of storytelling? It's mythology that has lasted so long. Nothing else has the same kind of staying power. What's the difference between mythology and religion? Mythology is somebody else's religion?"

"Right," I say. My eyes flick to Rumi and then back to Thalia. I imagine the bright colors of my big book of Greek mythology. The weight of it on my lap. "It's also that the stories, they make me feel safe. You know?"

"Me too," Thalia says. We're both quiet and then she notices me noticing Rumi and her face settles into disapproval, a deep crease between her straight-across brows.

I feel my cheeks tingle and press my cold fingers to my hot

skin. I'm trying really hard to not look at Rumi, to not let Thalia see me looking, but also I stretch my legs out, long and tan, and I notice when his gaze graces my bare legs, my shoulders, my face. He smiles at me, behind the counter. I feel like he's touching me. And when he takes off his apron and comes and sits down at our table, I try to pretend the space between us doesn't tingle.

He touches my coffee mug. "Can I?" he says.

I nod and again I can feel Thalia's attention and I look down, away from Rumi drinking out of my cup. I imagine what his lips might feel like.

Thalia closes her computer with a snap. "I need to go to the store."

"Already?" I say.

"We were supposed to do it this morning but Dad had to do soccer stuff. The program director got into a car accident last week and he has to take over for her and he says it's been a nightmare. We're making braised short ribs and Dad needs pickling spices."

We used to cook together at Thalia's house. Things that would take all day. Things long and beautiful that filled the house with smells. Back when we were in third grade, fourth grade, something like that. Back when things were okay.

Her dad is outside, here to pick Thalia up. He's talking to the kids sitting on the sidewalk. He laughs about something and hands the girl with blue hair some money and she's smiling up at him, watching him as he opens the door. He comes over to say hi and ask us generic friend's-parent questions until they leave, his hand on Thalia's shoulder, steering her out the door.

Rumi is watching me watch them leave like he can see the inside of my brain. "Want to go somewhere?" he says.

My hands are under the table. I rub my middle finger with my thumb.

I should say no.

The sun is on my face, shining hot through the windows, and it lights up my eyes, making them glow, I think. It smells like coffee beans and there is a low chatter and the whir of espresso machines and nobody is looking at us. I think about leaning in and I see him glance at my lips, and I want him to come close enough to smell my perfume.

"Escape?" he says. Like he's rescuing me from a tower.

I'm just pretending anyway. This is all pretend.

We pick raspberries. His aunt runs a community garden behind the Dick's Drive-In in Wallingford. We walk even though it's too far and we have to cross over the freeway. It's on their property like a massive backyard with aisles of vines and pumpkin plants oozing like lava over tires painted bright colors and filled with summer blooms. An old man with a straw hat digs his bare hands into a patch of lettuce and nods at us as we go by. There are families and sweethearts picking berries with stained red fingers and sunshine in their hair.

Mostly I just pick and eat. The berries are bursting and warm and I am hungry. I realize it's been a while since I consumed anything other than coffee or alcohol.

So far we haven't talked much. He hasn't mentioned Poppy and neither have I even though I feel a strange ache, wondering where she is. He just hosts me here in this bright garden. Rumi smiles a lot, not at me. Like he's trying not to look at me too often. But at the creeping green sweet-smelling raspberry vines. At the other people, whose voices seem muffled. He looks at my hands, lingering on the berries and when I push my hair out of my face. I wish I had a hair tie.

"Here," he says. He gathers my hair. His fingers are calloused and rough. They brush the back of my neck. He twists my hair into a knot. I can't see what he pulls out of his pocket, and he slides it in, securing the knot.

"What was that? That you put in?"

He rests his hand on the nape of my neck, then moves around so I can see his face. "A pencil, from The Pearl. I'm a frequent accidental pencil thief."

I think of Thalia for some reason and the way it felt to look at her and remember me and Edison.

"Lyra!" Rumi yells, looking over my shoulder. An adolescent girl with warm ocher skin like Rumi's and dark straight hair comes out of the house, yanking a puppy on a way-too-long leash. Rumi waves her over.

"He shit on the carpet again!" she says. She's wearing black high-tops with the laces untied.

"She's going to make you get rid of him," Rumi says.

The dog is small and brown with floppy ears and a docked

tail. His whole body is wiggly and excited as he sniffs my feet. She sits on the ground and pulls him into her lap and tries to hug him while he struggles to paint her face with his tongue. "I don't care. I'm never getting rid of him. I love him."

Rumi sighs and laughs and says to me, "This is my sister, Lyra, and her dumb dog, Trunks."

Lyra coos into the dog's neck, "Oh, are you a dumb dog? You beautiful dumb dog."

"Trunks, as in *Dragon Ball*?" I say to Rumi.

"Right, she's in a phase."

"An anime phase, I presume."

He nods and laughs and I'm sort of ready for Lyra to go away but she vibrates along next to us as we pick berries. "I'm using this app on my phone," she says, and I'm wondering why she's talking to me. "On my iPhone. I have an iPhone." She looks at me and I nod and smile, pretending to be impressed. Rumi is up ahead and I think he's listening. "And I used this app to make a stop-motion movie with my Legos. I have this Lego movie kit, but also I'm using my Star Wars Legos, but I changed it to Dark Sky instead of Darth Vader because of copyright and I don't want to get, like, sued."

"Right," I say.

"Do you want to see it?"

Rumi lifts his chin up a little and I think he's waiting to hear my answer. I think he's hoping that I'll say yes. And I feel a pang thinking of the pang *he* might feel for his sister who wants to show me her stupid video. So I smile. "Yes, definitely."

She runs off to get her phone. We walk behind her and Rumi

takes my hand. I know we shouldn't because how would I, how could I explain this to Poppy? I couldn't. But his hand is warm and rough and I don't want to let go.

The video is stunningly bad. I can see the corner of her finger for most of it, blocking the hiccupping action of the little Lego men who just do not emote particularly well. It's kind of like one of those old silent movies with the scene and then the words coming next, in this case in lopsided and scrunched-up handwriting that I can't really read. But Rumi has this big smile on his face watching me watch the video. So does Lyra.

It's over now and I look at her and her face is so wide-open. "That was great! Really great. Is it like a series? Because I'm not sure that little Lego guy is out of trouble. That other little Lego guy looks like he might be coming back for revenge."

"Yeah, I mean my friend really likes them too. He told me to keep sending them, so I think I'll be doing more episodes, like maybe three a day," Lyra says.

I get into Rumi's brick-like Volvo with my flat of raspberries. The world is somehow both orange and blue, dusky and dusty in the twilight, and it's getting cold. He turns on the heat and drives me home. The lights are on when we pull into the driveway. But it's quiet and I think going inside is an acceptable risk.

My fingers are on the cardboard flat and it's cool on my legs. "They smell good," I say. "The raspberries."

"Yeah?" Rumi says. I can't read his smile. Is it something or is it nothing? It's nothing, of course. Because he's with Poppy.

So, "Thank you," I say. "Really." But I leave the raspberries in his car. I don't like to think about their luscious ripe red sitting on my sticky kitchen counter.

Inside, I stand at my bedroom window. I think of being with Rumi in the garden. In the sun and the warm and the wind.

It doesn't matter anyway. I don't expect to see Rumi like this again. I just don't. I can't.

I left my pipe at Poppy's. I really want it and it's not even nine yet. I text her again, and again she doesn't respond.

I scroll up and up and it's all just me, acting casual, telling jokes, memes, GIFs, then: *where are you? seriously where are you? Poppy? are you mad at me? wtf is going on?*

I text her again: *i left my pipe there want to get high? ill give you greens.*

But nothing.

There are lights on in her house. Glowing warm squares. Like a lantern in the vast night, guiding me, calling me home.

Is she there and just ignoring me?

It's just an excuse. I mean, I really do want my pipe. But I also want to know what's going on. To see Poppy.

Willow answers the door, and rests one bare foot on top of the other, toes painted mint green.

"I forgot something," I say.

She stands back from the door. "Sure, come on in, Virginia." She leans against the counter. I remember when they reno- vated. Me and Poppy took sledgehammers to the wall between the kitchen and the dining room, wearing safety glasses and ponchos, Willow laughing and taking photos of us. Now it's open and bright and white. Willow says, "Want some tea? I just put the kettle on."

"I mean," I say, thumbing over my shoulder, "is Poppy here? I'll just go up."

Willow opens her mouth and then closes it again.

The kettle starts hissing steam.

"She didn't tell you?" Willow says.

"Tell me what?"

The kettle screams and she yanks it off the stove. "Poppy went to stay with my dad," Willow says, turning back to me.

"For how long?"

"Virginia," Willow says.

Her eyes are so light brown, they're almost gold. The worst part is watching her watch me, knowing that she sees the realization on my face. That all is not right here.

"The whole summer," Willow says. "She'll be back in September."

I take a step back. The rug is thick and soft under my feet.

"It was really last minute. He's been asking her to come stay for a while but she just decided to go."

I turn to leave.

"Don't you need your thing?" Willow calls after me.

What thing? I can't remember.

My cheeks are hot. I wave over my shoulder, vague, embarrassed.

Poppy is gone.

Poppy is gone and she's not coming back for the whole summer and I don't . . .

I don't

know

how

to

exist

without her.

*O*nce upon a time there was this beautiful woman. Her name was Fatima. And once upon a time there was this rich man with a blue beard and a castle. Fatima didn't know him, like at all, but her father said okay when Blue Beard asked if he could marry her because why not? He was rich and he had a castle, so they got married. And his castle was beautiful, that much was true. And he had many servants, that was true too. And Fatima thought she might be happy with her rich husband and beautiful castle and many servants. She would live happily ever after, right?

But then Fatima heard the rumors of lost wives. The wives who came before her. The wives who disappeared. Would she be one more lost wife? Would another lost wife come after her? But she had nobody to talk to. Nobody to ask, What happened to them? Nobody to ask, What will happen to me? She was alone.

Blue Beard traveled often, and after all, she was his wife, so he gave her the keys to his castle. And she wandered and talked to no one and in her wanderings she found a plain black door at the bottom of the castle and then Blue Beard found her at the plain black door. Never never never open that door, he raged. Fatima was frightened and she ran to her own chamber and hid until he left on an errand. But like she had no will of her own, she felt herself drawn again and again to the door.

She stood and stared at the door, black and small. As
though she could see through the wood, she stared.
As though she could open it with her eyes, she stared.
Why didn't he want her to? What was in there? It called
to her. Open, open, open, it said. So finally she did.

Shivering in the darkness were the corpses of her
predecessors. A bloody reaching arm, a stretched white
grin, staring eyes and rolled-back eyes and rotted graying
eyes. She stood there staring into the abyss and the abyss
stared back.

Five

I DREAM OF empty space. The void between the stars.

At first, though, I didn't. I couldn't sleep. My eyes ached. My heart. It ached too.

I texted Ro, Paz, Thalia. *poppy left,* I said. *shes gone for the whole summer and shes not answering any of my texts.*

wtf, Ro said.

Really? Paz said.

Why? Thalia said.

But I didn't know what to say and I couldn't sleep, so I lulled myself to sleep with crimson lullabies and drowning red, wine, wine, wine down my throat, sour and left open from two nights ago when my mom forgot about it and so I swallowed it and swallowed it.

Until everything tilted and spun and I could blank out black out black everything out.

. . .

I don't have Poppy's house to escape to. Not at all. Not just one night. Not just trying to get through one or two nights. She's just not here.

The alarm going off feels like somebody stabbing me behind the eyeball. I try to convince myself that it won't be so bad as I get dressed in what might seem like appropriate tutor attire to a parent who is not looking so closely. But I need money for the bus and for cups of coffee and for those hum bao rolls they sell in Pike Place and also for that rose-flavored Turkish delight too.

The community center is full of windows—that is to say, very bright. I guzzle coffee and Excedrin as a libation to the Hangover Gods and hope for the best. Langston is sitting on a bench with a book in his face. *The Return of the King.*

"So you're still a nerd," I say.

He glances at me with a sideways smile. He really is very handsome. He looks like a darker-skinned Michael B. Jordan, including the dimples. "How many times have you read *The Lord of the Rings*, anyway?"

"Including *The Hobbit*?"

I shrug.

"Either way, a lot." He straightens up. "It's like comfort food, you know? I know it so well by now, it's not challenging. It's just familiar and sweet." He marks his place and frowns at me. "What are you doing here?"

"I'm here to tutor. Doi."

The meeting room doors open and the milling parents and angsty middle schoolers file in and I see a small fidgeting figure, smiling and waving. It's Lyra. And I remember now that Rumi said she was getting tutored this summer.

Langston gets a look on his face, like he's actually happy to see all these kids, and I imitate him. Goddammit, I think Lyra is asking if I can tutor her.

"How's Trunks?" I say when she sits down across from me.

"Well, he ate the remote and also he peed in Aunt Jen's closet, that was last night, and this morning he peed right by the door on his way outside to pee."

"Oops," I say.

She shrugs. "My aunt got mad and yelled at me, and Rumi also got mad but he didn't yell."

She's struggling with the text-dependent analysis but I'm not supposed to help. She mouths words, sounding them out. She's reading at a fourth-grade level even though she's starting sixth next year. Her hair is unbrushed and her T-shirt is wrinkled with a purple stain on it. She gives me the impression of a little match girl, Oliver Twist, a boxcar child. Halfway homeless, a little bit of an orphan.

I read the sample page upside down. Some girl is watching the ocean waves and thinking about how they're beautiful and scary at the same time. Lyra drops her head on the table with a clunk and pretends to snore.

"I know it's dumb, but we have to do it," I say, and poke her shoulder. She rolls her head to the other side and snores even louder. Langston looks up from the next table and smiles at her and I roll my eyes at him.

When the session ends, Lyra and I walk outside together. Maybe it's not the most professional-responsible-conventional thing to do, but I sit on the curb and Lyra sits down next to me, stretching her legs out into the parking lot. She sings a little to herself and I'm wishing she would just go already because I don't feel like sitting here with her and then she says, "I sneak out sometimes. I snuck out last night and went to a movie."

"Huh," I say, digging in my pocket looking for an emergency joint. Rumi smokes, I think. Maybe Lyra won't care. All the kids and parents are gone. Nobody's looking. I lean forward so my hair is shielding my face and light it.

"Can I have some?" Lyra asks.

"No."

She doesn't say anything and neither do I.

But then because it's so awkward I say, "What movie?"

"*Texas Chainsaw Massacre*," she says proudly. "They were doing a special."

"Gross." God, where's Rumi? Why am I sitting here with this sicko?

When he pulls up and she runs for his car, I wave to Rumi and follow her. He rolls down the window and smiles his one-dimpled smile.

"Have you heard from Poppy?" I ask.

He turns his phone over in his hands. "No," he says.

I lean on his open window, my elbows on the hot metal of

his car. He looks up at me and I realize how close we are. I feel it like a pulse, like a heartbeat, but I don't move back. "She's gone. She went to her grandpa's for the summer. Her mom told me last night. I keep trying to call her and she's not answering."

His mouth falls open.

"I know," I say. I know.

This sudden lack of her.

Does he feel it like I do? Like something was cut from him, carved from him?

Does he feel this strange sense of betrayal? She left without telling me. She left without saying goodbye.

What does that mean?

Does he ask himself? What does that mean?

I don't feel like going inside when I get home. I cut through the in-between yards and lie on a sunny patch of grass at the reservoir park.

I think about texting Poppy.

But I don't know what to say.

And she probably wouldn't answer anyway.

I think about texting her about Rumi. About how she left him too. But I don't do that either.

I flip over and stare past the grass, to the dirt and bugs beyond. I spend I-don't-know-how-long watching the ants and the aphids and the tiny I-don't-know-whats and their existence in the sunlight that is filtered and refracted by dewdrops.

It could be a regular day. We'll see each other, Poppy and me, in the afternoon. Before my parents come home. I'll be out of my house. I could spend the night with her if I need to.

But it's not.

When I text Ro, she comes. "Remember last summer?" she says, pushing her long brown legs against the gravel, pushing her body into the air behind. She nods toward the reservoir.

I swing with her. "When we skinny-dipped?"

"And those boys saw us?" she says.

"And we tried to put our bathing suits back on under our towels so they didn't realize we were actually naked?"

"Oh, they totally knew," Ro says.

"We weren't sneaky."

"But what a bunch of assholes though staring at us like that," she says.

"Paz!" I shout, waving. She climbs through the hedges between our cul-de-sac and the park and Thalia emerges behind her. Paz picks a leaf out of Thalia's hair and they both laugh.

"Remember skinny-dipping?" Ro says when they get close enough.

"And those assholes were spying on us?" Thalia says.

"Dicks," Paz says.

"And then we told Poppy's mom about it and she told us how she and her high school friends did the same thing only they were brazenly singing at the top of their lungs and jumping off the walls and not ashamed at all," I say.

Ro laughs. "That was awesome."

"I felt like less of a hooch," I say.

Paz and Thalia fight over who gets the last swing and Paz climbs on and then Thalia says, "Fine, let's spider." And she climbs on Paz's lap and faces the other way, sticking her legs out behind Paz's back, and they yank each other back and forth until they find their rhythm. And then Ro does this trick where she flips over herself in her swing and lands like Black Widow and when I try to imitate her, I get a mouthful of gravel and hair.

But then Ro has to go home for dinner.

And Paz and Thalia have movie tickets with Langston and Edison.

"I'd invite you, but my uncle is coming over and you know how my mom is," Ro says.

I nod. "Family time," I say.

And Paz says, "Sold-out theater." And she kisses me on the cheek.

And I swing with bravado, kicking my legs out, sailing my hair behind me, long body, sky flying, close my eyes, swing, swing, until they're gone. And then when they're all gone I stop swinging and sit there dangling, aimless feet making circles in the gravel.

The thing about my dad is that it doesn't need to be the weekend for him to party. It doesn't need to be a Friday night for him to get drunk with his friends.

I watch a spider crawl across my sparkling popcorn ceiling.

The spider moves so slow I have to look away, then look back again to measure his distance. Closer and closer he gets to the crack above my bed. Delicious sharp smoke circles through my lungs and I blow it out, aiming for the spider who I've named Anansi. Anansi and I are friends now and I'd like him to get high with me.

I hear my dad come home and he and my mom start yelling at each other. Why does he need so much beer? Why does he need all that liquor? He has to work in the morning.

Why does she have to be such a bitch? Why can't he just have fun without her nagging him all the fucking time?

I don't turn on my light but watch the sunlight fade to twilight fade to night.

Down the hall the TV goes on, then the music over it and then the knocks on the door start occurring and reoccurring voices and voices and voices and then I hear His voice and I thrust my window open and I pop out the screen and I drop down and I run and run and run so fast it's like I'm running for my life running scared from things that creep and things that chase.

I remember how it was before Poppy moved here. Like this. Like I was halfway homeless.

Lyra sneaks out, she says. Where does she go? Why does she want to be out on cold nights like this? She sneaks *out* and I just wish I had somewhere to sneak back *into*. Like when Poppy and me sneak out to dance through the park, light candles and cast spells, pick flowers and stick them in keyholes and fence post cracks and mailboxes and pretend we're fairies on May Day. And then we sneak back in and Willow probably knows and thinks it's sweet and wholesome and buys us the good bagels in the morning.

This isn't like that. Nobody knows where I am or what I'm doing. And Poppy is gone.

I'm tired now and it starts to rain just like when I was eleven. I text Paz and Ro but they don't respond. It's late. They're probably asleep.

It's been so long since anything happened. So I walk home and I feel like I'm giving up.

But I can't let myself sleep, not with Him downstairs. I stare at Anansi feeling like there's dust in my eyes. There's a slammed door and a crash and glass breaking. I'm not sure if my parents are fighting or if my dad is stumbling around drunk and knocking things over or if the guys are brawling over a disputed win or if somebody broke into our house and they're trashing it for fun.

I just want to sleep.

But what if while I sleep He comes in? He might. Even though He hasn't in so long. He might tonight.

I get up and jiggle the padlock that Poppy helped me install a few years ago. She doesn't know exactly why. She just knows I don't feel safe. It's a distinction I made. Like, *Haha maybe I'm just paranoid but you know I'd feel so much better if nobody could stumble in drunk to my room and mess with me in the middle of the night.*

I tug on my doorknob without making any noise so I don't draw attention to my door or my room or myself or any parts of myself. I get back in bed clutching the key to the lock.

Eventually the house goes quiet and the outside noises, the wind and the trees and the distant passing cars, become the only things I hear. Even though I know I shouldn't, I sleep.

It's so quiet, I'm not sure what woke me. I'm sitting up in bed and my heart is pounding.

Nothing.

It's so dark, I can't see.

Then, a sound.

What is it?

I can't see.

I strain through the darkness. It's my door. My doorknob is turning this way and that. The door is pushing against the padlock on the inside, somebody is trying to get in my room, I don't move I can't I can't draw attention to myself I'm just lying here sleeping please just go please please leave please go away.

After it's been quiet a long time I lie back down but I don't sleep.

Six

MY PHONE STARTS ringing at seven thirty.

The crashing started back up and my room was gray with predawn light and the noise meant somebody else was awake. And so I felt safe, a bit more safe anyway, than in the darkest, quietest part of the night. And my eyes were itchy and sandy and hot and dry and so I managed to sleep for a little while, I guess.

And anyway Rumi calls me at seven thirty.

I lurch to the phone trying to shut it the fuck up and he starts talking about a music festival he's got tickets to. Langston flaked out on him and Janelle Monáe is playing and can I go it will be awesome.

I clear my throat. "Sure," I say.

"Are you okay?"

I search for Anansi and find him plump in the middle of his web. "Just tired."

"Well, drink some coffee and get dressed."

"Okay." Anansi wiggles his legs.

"I'll be around to pick you up in an hour."

I fall back asleep for approximately forty-five minutes. Rumi is ten minutes early.

I've got my big sunglasses on, my hair in a knot, and I'm

wearing the leggings and tank top I slept in. In the mirror on my way out I look like a vacant house. There's a tiny shape staring out of one of the blank windows. That's my face. I pinch my cheeks, run down the stairs to Rumi's car, trying to look okay.

We find parking so far away we might as well have not driven. "We should have just taken the bus," I say, and Rumi shrugs.

"I like walking with you," he says, and his hand brushes mine as it swings.

It's all just pretend. I'm just pretending.

First things first, we get some fair food. Elephant ears, pad Thai, lemonade with a whole half a lemon floating in the ice cubes. I lie on the grass and absorb the sun and let it fill up the empty space inside me. Rumi sits crisscross-applesauce next to me and prattles. I'm only kind of following until he mentions Edison.

I guess he notices my reaction, because he pauses. "What's going on with you guys anyway?" he says.

"Come on, like you don't know."

His face is blank.

"Everybody knows I'm That Kind of Girl." I feel like an idiot as I say it. It's a stupid cliché thing to say and it doesn't properly describe the way I feel about myself.

But it's true. Everybody knows. Everybody knows that I had sex for the first time when I was fourteen and with a college guy who didn't even know how old I was. Everybody knows I gave Isaiah a hand job in the bathroom at Green Lake that one time. Everybody knows I've cheated on every boyfriend I've ever had.

Rumi leans back. "What kind of girl is that?"

The sun is hot and the crowd wanders around us, cloaked in smoke and feathers and scarves and sandals, and music from four or five different concerts blends together into a lovely kind of white noise.

And I don't know why this time I decide to tell my version of the story. The one that actually happened. Maybe because he's not friends with Thalia. Because he won't feel divided between us. Maybe because I'm warm and the sun is golden and it's in my face and I feel like Rumi's actually, really looking at me.

"Once upon a time," I say, and smile at Rumi like I know I'm being silly. His return smile is small. "Once upon a time I accidentally let myself be alone in a room with Edison. It was a party at Isaiah's house. I needed to pee and used the master bath and he followed me in. I don't know why, but I kind of flirted with him. I mean, sometimes I think that's the only way I know how to relate to guys. I sat on the bed and he sat next to me. The door was still open, but just a crack. And then he kept doing this thing where he tried to kiss me."

Rumi is in the corner of my eye, but I keep watching the crowds. "And like I didn't want to hurt his feelings and I didn't want him to think I'm a bitch. But he kept trying to kiss me and I'd laugh and you know, turn my head or whatever and I was trying to be chill about it but he, he just wouldn't stop. So finally I let him kiss me. And. He just kept kissing me. I remember this moment when somebody went by the door on the outside and they were laughing really loud and I wanted so much for them to come in, whoever it was, and interrupt us. I just couldn't figure out how to get myself out of there. I remember staring at the door, hoping it would open all the way. Like my whole existence, my whole self was in my eyes staring at that door."

I sigh and push my fingertips to my forehead. "And then it's like I had to make myself like it or at least act like I liked it because I didn't want him to think I'm frigid. And then he put my hand on his dick over his pants and I knew how it was going to end."

Rumi won't look at me.

"We didn't do it, but I did give him head. And then I could finally leave and I don't know if anybody at the party knew, but they might have."

He still won't look at me. So he thinks of me differently now than he used to. So what. So does everybody.

"And anyway, that's it." I look past his shoulder, but it's all blurs now. And so it's just that terrible quiet.

I don't know how long we sit like this before he turns and his eyes glow in a brilliant pulse of sunset and suddenly I realize how much I care what he thinks. How much I want him to think of me as just Virginia, not Virginia-who-fucks-anybody.

"I'm so sorry that happened to you," he says.

"What?"

"Edison. I'm so sorry."

"I don't know what you're talking about."

His expression changes ever so slightly. "It doesn't sound, like, consensual."

I don't say anything because my throat is starting to hurt and my eyes feel hot and I don't know what to say.

"I mean, Virginia, the way you described it, it sounds like sexual assault," he says.

"Edison assaulted you," he says.

"Virginia?" he says.

I feel a tear spill over and run down my cheek but I ignore it because I don't want Rumi to notice, so I look the other way and bite my lip as hard as I can to stop myself from crying.

Rumi shifts, not close enough to touch, but I can feel his warmth now. "Virginia, are you okay?"

I give myself one more second.

He's frowning, leaning close.

"I'm fine," I say.

"Are you?"

But I don't answer.

When I get home I sit in the dark on the front steps and watch Rumi drive away and I hold my phone in my hands and stare at his name in my contact list. I think about deleting him. I think about blocking him.

I run my thumb along his contact picture.

I don't do either.

I go inside and upstairs, snatching a bottle of wine along the way.

I text Ro, but she's got family time. Paz is with Langston. Thalia doesn't answer.

Why did I tell Rumi? I look at the photos I took of him at the concert. Smoke and sunbeams, blurred lines, colors running together like wet paint. He smiles, looking through the camera right at me. It's the way he looks at me. It's the way he sees me. It's the way he saw what really happened between me and Edison. What I didn't have the words for but in my gut I knew. He gave me the words. It wasn't consensual, he said.

Lyra is writing a story. I resist the urge to look at my phone. She's frowning and then writing and then laughing and then writing some more. She slides the paper across the table when she's done. I think she's trying not to smile.

I clear my throat and start reading:

THE TRAGIC DEMICE OF IMOGEN BLACK

Once upon a time there was a kid named Imogen Black. She was a Girl Scout and she cared more then anything at all about selling alot of cookies. But her mom and dad were both dead and she had nobodys help. The grocery stores didnt let her sit outside and sell her cookies because she didnt have a grown up with her and also neither did the gas stations. She asked her teachers to buy them but they all yelled NO WE CANT BECAUSE THATS NOT PROFSIONAL! So she tried one last time and the mcdonalds let her try to sell her cookies but evrytime anybody walked by they said NO WE DONT WANT ANY COOOKIES WE JUST WANT BURGERS AND FRYS! And so imogen decided to eat all the cookies and she choked on one and died the end.

I stare at the paper and then I start laughing. Langston looks at me from across the room and I realize I'm laughing really loud. I cover my mouth with my hands. Lyra is watching me and laughing a little too. I take out my red pen that I'm supposed to correct all her grammar and spelling and punctuation with and write *A++++++ 100%* and say, "It's perfect. I love it."

"Really?" she says, trying to suppress her smile.

"Yes really really a lot." I look at the paper for another minute and I say, "Can I keep it?"

She blushes and nods, pink staining her bronze cheeks like spilled ink.

After tutoring we walk out together. I say, "So, you like anime?"

She scuffs her Converse on the sidewalk and shrugs.

"Like how you named your dog Trunks? That's after that *Dragon Ball* character, right?"

"*Dragon Ball Z.*"

"Why do you like him?"

Finally she smiles. "He's really like funny and strong and I like that he starts off really like conceited but then is also really good at fighting and he gets like less conceited as time goes on. And I want my Trunks to be smart like that, and so maybe he'll stop peeing everywhere all the time."

Rumi is leaning against his car with his hands in his pockets like he's the heartthrob in some eighties movie. And it kind of works. My heart literally throbs. "Hey," I say.

He smiles at me. "Hey."

"Have you heard from Poppy?" This time when I ask him it

feels a bit less like an ache, less like a strange kind of desperate hope and more like I already know the answer and I just want to get it out of the way.

He shakes his head looking down at the ground and then back up at me and my heart throbs again. Heartthrob, I think at him and smile.

"What?" he says, quirking his head like he heard my thought.

"Nothing," I say, still smiling, and I wave at Rumi as he pulls away.

I walk to Ro's house and Suzanna, her mom, lets me in. She has a distracted look on her face and she says, "Ramona's not here but you can go on up, baby. Don't mind me, I'm working on this piece for the *Times* and I . . ." She wanders over to her computer at the kitchen table without finishing her sentence. Ro says Suzanna's working on a story that's really messing with her. About these girls who got sexually assaulted at the University and reported it and then nothing happened. One of them even dropped out because she kept ending up in classes with her rapist.

I climb into Ro's bed to wait for her, and the soft pillows and the soft sheets and the safety lull me to sleep. She comes blazing in and wakes me up. "Party! Tonight. Now. Up."

"Why so punctuated?" I say, rolling into the pillow and trying to ignore her.

She yanks the pillow out from under my head and throws the blankets on the floor.

I curl up against the chill. "Why is it so cold in here?"

"Air-conditioning. Get out of bed. It's warm and wonderful outside."

"I'm not in the mood, Ro."

Ro climbs in and puts her arms around me and pulls me close so I can smell her limoncello lotion. "It'll be fun. You haven't been out since that party at Isaiah's. Come on, get up. Bon courage."

"You stay here. We don't need the rest of them."

"Hah."

I turn a sigh into a raspberry against her neck and she shrieks, leaping up and throwing a sock at me. I already know she's going to win and I'm going to give in, so I start fixing my makeup, borrowing Ro's purple eyeliner.

"Alien Barbie!" Ro says, holding the doll up.

"She was under your bed, poor thing."

Ro peels off the fake-Barbie's plastic face, revealing the weird duck lips underneath, and wiggles her at me. "Let's put her on the roof."

We climb out Ro's window onto the gable. There's a pipe sticking out of the shingles. It's rusted and mossy and I don't know what it's for. Ro hands me Alien Barbie and I stick her butt into the pipe so she's splayed out and lounging, waiting for her alien overlords to come back and get her. Ro puts her peeled-off face on her lap and I fix her hair.

"Fare thee well, Alien Barbie," Ro says. "I hope you finally get to go home." We've been putting her on the roof since we were little.

I scoot to the edge of the roof. "Should we just jump?"

"Gah," Ro says, but then she grins at me and leaps off the roof. I shriek and jump down after her and we tumble onto the grass together.

Ro ties my hair back in a scrunchie from around her wrist and we run together out of the cul-de-sac. The road curves away and we walk up the hill. An old woman comes jogging around the corner. She is fat and tan and wearing neon booty shorts and a headband on her curly old-lady hair. She huffs her breath out and out and out, her head down and her cheeks red. Even from here I can see how hard she is working. I feel a pang, missing the strain of muscles, the searing breath, the sweat.

A pickup truck charges down the road and the guys in the back scream at the old woman. I can't understand them, it's just a jumble of fucks and olds and I turn the other way as the screaming assaults me.

"Gross," Ro says.

They're going to the party. I recognize guys from my school. Edison is hanging over the tailgate and we make eye contact and he lifts his arms up and bellows my name. I scream back and start running and ignore Ro calling my name and then all the guys in the truck start yelling and pumping their fists in the air and I truly sprint now and for a second I feel exhilarated and unbeatable. I catch up to the truck and the guys sitting in the bed reach out their hands to me. I take a running leap and grab their hands and vault into the bed with my foot propelling my body into the air off the bumper. I am received with fuck yeahs and high fives and somebody pushes an open can of beer into my hand and I chug it, a little dribbling down my chin.

The old woman is still running. Her pace didn't change at all, despite the yelling and cursing and degrading. She jogs along a gentle curve and disappears behind some trees and I wish I were with her.

I free myself from Edison even though he's clutching at me. Ro catches up when I'm at the house. She rolls her eyes at me so hard she probably gives herself a headache. Ro's texting Thalia and Paz to find out where they are and if they're at the party yet and then we go around back to where some juniors made a fire and warm our hands under the spark-and-smoke-filled sky.

"I've never had an orgasm," Thalia is saying. She's sitting on a plastic striped beach chair clutching a chipped mug with a bunch of boobs painted on it.

"Not even by yourself?" Paz says.

"Nope."

"Have you ever used a vibrator?" Ro asks.

"No." Thalia shrugs.

"You should try," I say. "The first time I had an orgasm was when I got that vibrator." I look at Ro. "Remember when we bought it?"

She laughs. "Yeah."

"I thought you had an orgasm with that one dude," Thalia says.

I bought the vibrator at this sex toy store called Babes in Toyland. Ro was giggling and I was faking sophistication. As if

I knew exactly how my clit worked and where my G spot was and if it even existed. I said I'd had an orgasm from penetration. The shop girl gave me the benefit of the doubt and guided me toward a display of long, thin, twisted things with bulbous heads, like shiny pretty penises.

In the middle of the day when my parents were at work I held it over my underwear and pressed it hard against my clit and strained and gasped and held my legs rigid and finally felt wave after wave of something indescribable. I remember feeling close to tears, close to God, close to my own self.

That was the first time I had an orgasm but that's not what I told Thalia or Paz or even Poppy. I lied and said my ex-boyfriend gave me orgasms all the time. All the orgasms. He could practically make me come just by rubbing my boobs or kissing my neck.

"That was a lie." I shrug. "I felt like my ability or inability to have an orgasm reflects on how, I don't know, feminine I am, you know?"

Ro is nodding and Thalia is looking the other way and I stutter on. "Like, if it's hard to make me come that means I'm frigid or something. Like having an orgasm is a part of my job as a sexual partner."

"Yeah, like being able to orgasm really easily makes you this easygoing, relaxed, functional person and if you can't it's your fault, not theirs," Ro says.

Paz shrugs. She struggles and then shrugs again. "Yeah, I mean my perspective might be different because I'm trans and maybe my perception of my role in society is different, like subtly? I'm not sure. Also, I mean I've been on hormones since I was twelve but it's hard to say exactly how it affects my ability to orgasm versus your ability to orgasm, but I guess you could say that about any two women. I mean everybody is different, you know?"

"But you've had an orgasm?" Thalia asks Paz.

"Well, yeah."

"What's wrong with me?" Thalia wails.

"I've actually never had an orgasm with a guy," I admit. "I feel really strange about it. What if I can't, like ever?"

For a minute it's quiet while we contemplate this strange thing that me and Thalia have in common. It just sits in the middle of our group. I am looking at her and she's not looking at me.

And then Ro jumps in. She says to Thalia, "Most people have no idea what they're doing at this age and especially if you've never tried with a vibrator it's not that unusual."

"You've never had an orgasm with Edison?" Paz says.

"I mean it feels good." Thalia starts to scramble. "But I just, I don't really like it when he goes down on me." She takes a long drink.

"Really?" Ro says.

Paz shakes her head. "I just don't know why you're with him."

I am scrupulously quiet but Thalia glances at me anyway before she says, "It's just, it's complicated." She wraps her arms around her waist.

"You're too good for him, Thalia," I say accidentally-on-purpose, and as soon as the words are out of my mouth I feel exposed and stupid.

Thalia doesn't respond, she just takes another drink. Swallow swallow swallow. Ro says something to Paz and they laugh, but I'm not paying attention.

"Has anybody heard from Poppy?" I ask.

Paz looks at me and then Ro and then finally Thalia. We all spend a minute just staring and waiting for somebody to say something.

"Do you think she's okay?" Thalia asks.

But nobody has the answer.

I wind up in the kitchen, taking shots and shotgunning beers. I've lost Paz, and Thalia puked behind a bush in the backyard and Ro left with her, making sure she got home. And now here is Edison and he touches the small of my back in a way that feels intimate and invasive but nobody can see, I don't think. My back is to the wall. I smile at him and try to think of an excuse to leave. To go find Ro, to bring Paz a beer, to go outside and make a phone call. But now he touches my belly, slips his hand beneath my shirt, his fingers on my bare skin. I see it when Isaiah notices, when his eyebrows quirk and he smirks at Edison. I laugh like it's no big deal, he's just drunk, he's just flirting. I leave with a feeble excuse like, *I have to pee*, but Edison follows and with every step he seems less concerned with people noticing.

So we leave together because I don't want to fuck in the bathroom.

We go to his dad's apartment. His room is messy and there are stains on his sheets and socks under his bed and it smells like mildew and sweat and I know as Edison pulls down his pants that I don't want to be here.

His boxers are off now.

He's lying back against his pillow looking at me expectantly.

His dick is out and it's hard and he's rolling on a condom.

I really don't want to be here.

I smile and shimmy out of my shorts and climb on the bed.

I lie on Edison's floor. I don't want to be in bed with him anyway. I straighten my shirt and pull up my underwear and my shorts. Edison's long bony foot dangles next to my head.

I think of Rumi. I think of his garden. I think of our almost kiss.

"I have to go," I say.

Edison barely looks up from his phone, glowing on his face.

I want to be brave, to say I'm done, to say Thalia doesn't deserve this, to say even I don't deserve this, I don't want it anymore. But I'm not brave. I just leave. And I hope that he won't call me ever again even though I know he will.

*O*nce upon a time there was this warrior woman. Her name was Aife. She lived in the hills of a windswept island that smelled like brine and heavy sky. Her sister lived in the Fortress of Shadows, five days' walk. Sometimes Aife walked it, after many weeks of feasting on shellfish and boar, when her body was strong and rested. She walked alongside her Ferghana horses, fed on oats and barley and wild grasses, instead of riding, so they would be strong and rested as well. (This isn't a good story.)

When she arrived there, at the Fortress of Shadows, she and her sister brawled and fought and battled and it was great fun. Her sister, Scáthach, thought she was the strongest and the fastest and the fiercest, but she wasn't. Aife was. And they fought to prove who was best, so Aife wasn't allowed to fight on her chariot led by her Ferghana horses because that would give her an unfair advantage according to Scáthach. Aife agreed because she didn't want her victory to be questioned when she won.

In the warm and salty summer sunshine, Aife fought Scáthach's champion. His name was Cú Cuchlainn. He was weak but he thought he was strong. Even though it was not her favorite to fight with swords, she almost had him. She could feel his heart beating at the end of her sword. Then he cried out and pointed behind her where *she couldn't see. He said her horses and her chariot were falling over the bluff into the ocean, and she turned and he overpowered her. (This is a bad story, a sad story.)*

As Aife bled with his sword on her neck, Cú Cuchlainn said he would let her live if she bore him a son. Aife elbowed him in the face and stomped on his foot and he gripped her tighter, hard against his body. His breath was hot on her ear and she could smell his sweat. He pressed his sword so hard on her throat that she couldn't breathe, so she only nodded because she didn't want to die. (I told you this isn't a good story.)

It took many tries before she got pregnant. But she did it because she wanted to live. She didn't want him touching her, fucking her, raping her. Her strong body wasn't hers anymore. She grieved for the warrior woman who would fight and be free. She wanted it to be over. She wanted it to be done so she could go. So she could be free and strong again. (She did not live happily ever after.)

Seven

IT'S MISTING RAIN and cold. I walk up the hill but the buses only run every hour now, so I call Paz because I know she'll come and get me. Even though it's late her parents are still up hosting a bunch of academics. They're professors at the university. Paz's mom waves at us as we scurry through the clumps of people and climb up to Paz's room.

"Want to play Mario?" she says, turning on her TV.

I shrug and climb onto her bed in the corner, under a sloping wood-paneled ceiling. It's like being on the inside of a ship. I run my finger along the hearts we've carved and initials and swirls on the wall, behind her blankets and pillows where her parents maybe haven't noticed yet.

"So," Paz says. She pokes weed into the bowl of her pipe. "Langston decided he's going to apply to UBC. And I mean, I know he'll get in." She does an excited little shimmy and hands me the pipe. "You get greens."

"So you guys will be only like two hours away!" Paz is going to the University since that's where her parents teach.

She jumps on a mushroom with her Mario, clacking the controller and leaning to the left, and then she says, "And I mean it works because they have a really good children's literature department or whatever."

I hand her the pipe. "Why kid lit?"

"He wants to be a children's librarian."

"Oh my god that's so adorable I might actually puke."

Her smile is so deep and bright it makes me ache. "I'm so glad he's going to be close. I mean, we might break up anyway and we're just in high school and we'll probably break up eventually, I mean, we're seventeen, it's not like we're getting married or anything."

I nod and nod and nod.

"Anyway, it's just I'm really glad we can stay together at least for now. He'll be able to come down for the weekends, you know?"

We lapse into silence and pass the pipe back and forth and I watch Paz try to dodge that evil sun that zooms around and then she dies and tosses the controller down.

"You know, I've had lots of sex," I say.

Paz nods, her expression neutral.

"But I feel like I've never been intimate like you and Langston."

She nods again and climbs into bed next to me and doesn't say anything.

"I wish I had that."

She lies back, her hair mingling with mine. "Love you," she says.

I smile. "Love you too."

Eventually I ask Paz if I can spend the night. It's okay because it's been a while and it's summer and her parents are up late anyway.

I lie next to Paz after she falls asleep. The wind is drifting in her open window.

I roll over and stare at my phone in my hand. I think about words and images zooming from my phone to other phones. Words and images, thoughts and feelings.

I take a picture of the full moon, hanging heavy and luscious in the lustrous dark sky. I send it to Rumi and bravely I type: *thinking of you.*

In the morning when I get home I dump out the old coffee and make some new and when it's ready I pour it into the mug Thalia made back in ninth grade, shiny blue glaze dripping onto the bare pale ceramic. It was one of those surprising accidents. She didn't know what she was doing when she painted it. She was messing around and then it turned out beautiful and we were both so enamored with it and then she gave it to me. And I love it.

I wipe the spilled sugar, the rings of coffee, the evidence of my existence off the counter and take my coffee to my room. White walls and gray air and posters hung crooked and photos taped to the walls. My bed is unmade and my box spring is showing. I straighten my purple quilt so it hides the dust under my bed. I fluff my limp pillow. I close my underwear drawer and turn off my yellow overhead light and open the window and I smell the clean bright air coming in and I pretend I'm somewhere else, drinking black coffee and reading science articles about nebulas and dwarf planets. My parents are at work and the house is empty and quiet.

There's a knock on the front door and I just know.

It's Rumi, holding a box. His smile is like a sunbeam.

"What is it?" I ask.

"Open it."

I unfold the cardboard top. It smells like dirt and bursting sweetness. It's fruit. Luscious jewel-bright fruit. Strawberries, raspberries, Rainier cherries. Rumi's fingers bear the stain of juice and washed-off dirt. My heart ripens a little.

"Did you?"

"I just picked them this morning. They're still warm from the sun." He hands me a bag too, filled with potatoes and zucchinis and blue-and-green-and-brown-speckled eggs.

I step back into the shadows of my house. "Won't you come in?" I say with a posh accent. Just pretending just pretending just pretending.

He wanders around my room. He touches my purple quilt. Runs his finger along the stitching. He looks out the window at the dogwood tree whose branches cover the sun. He picks up a picture, me and Poppy, surrounded by umbrellas, glowing red, blue, rainbow circles. We're crouching in a tree.

"The umbrellas were our fort," I say. Poppy's grin glows white in the photo. My pale skin reflects the light of the umbrellas so I look a little yellow, a little blue, a little red.

Rumi smiles down at it and then puts it back on the windowsill, gentle with the frame. He bends to peer at another photo I have tacked on the wall. This one is just me. We were at Cannon Beach for Poppy's sixteenth birthday. I'm in the water up to my knees, turned halfway to the side, smiling up into the sky.

"You can't see it, but there was a puffin. That's what I was looking at."

"There's puffins there?" he says.

"Isn't it amazing? I didn't know either."

"Can I have this?" He looks up at me, earnest.

"You want it?"

"You look so happy," he says.

"I was."

"So, can I?"

"Yes. Yeah. Yes, you can have it."

"Is that weird?" he says, laughing.

"I don't know," I say. "A little?"

He flicks the edge of the photo, looking down at it.

"But I like that you want it," I say.

We make the eggs and zucchini Rumi brought, and the potatoes are hot and a little raw and buttery with herbs. He stands behind me, moves beside me. The space between us is small and charged. He brushes my elbow, then my arm, then his fingertips linger on my waist.

Just pretending.

Touch me touch me touch me.

Just playing house.

I delve into my supply of Mom's wine. "Want some?" I slurp.

"I don't drink."

I think back and can't remember. "When did you quit?"

"I just never did. I mean, I choose not to."

I wonder, but I don't ask.

I really want him to stay. I wonder when he's going to say he has to go. He smiles when he catches me looking at him. "What?" he says.

"Your one dimple. It's, like, offensive."

"Offensive?" He laughs and covers his cheek with his hand.

This time though we don't talk about Poppy.

We fill up the space she left behind.

I drink more wine. He touches my wrist and I set the bottle down.

I look at him, at his startling ocean-green eyes and his dark hair just long enough to curl around his earlobe, at his face, his lips, his whole self. He wraps his hands around my wrists and I am thinking, what the fuck am I doing? And I'm also thinking, touch me, kiss me, hold me.

"Let's go outside," I say.

There is an oak tree, tall and arching for the sky. There is a spot between the tree and the fence. I am brave. I take Rumi's hand and lead him into the shadows. We lie beneath the sun behind the leaves. I bask in his presence and in the filtered light, in all its whiteness and all its blue.

We tell secrets.

I whisper, "I'm afraid of the dark."

He whispers back, "Why?"

And I tell him. "I forget, during the day, when I'm surrounded by people and noise and life. And then at night when everything goes dark and dead, I know there is nobody who cares what happens to me. I just can't let myself sleep. I feel like I need to watch to make sure nothing bad happens."

"What kinds of bad things happen in the dark?"

Our eyes catch and hold.

"Haven't you ever heard about my dad's parties?"

He doesn't answer. There is brief contact, a warmth of his skin on mine somewhere close and sweet. Then he says, "You can stay with me."

"Just whenever?"

"Yeah, just whenever."

In this moment I want to love him. There is a drumbeat in my heart. There is music on my skin. I want to share it with him. Why is love such a little word?

The day ebbs into night. We wander inside.

The way we end up in my bed is almost accidental.

First it's just my foot touching his. I rest the bottoms of my polished toes against the tops of his stockinged ones. Then my leg bravely entwines with his. As we talk, my hands fluttering in the air, he lifts my shoulders up, cradling my head, his arm secure around me, and I breathe into his chest.

Breathe in,

breathe out.

And we are silent.

I know what I'm feeling. I know what I want. Not what is expected of me, not what I feel pressured into, not what I feel like I have to pretend that I want.

What I actually finally want.

His proximity washes over me and it's intoxicating and I don't even think about it. I slip my leg up and over and then I'm straddling him, one arm on either side, my hands on the bed, his body hard beneath me, my hair falling in a curtain around our faces.

We are so close.

He smiles a little and he runs his hands up my arms, tangles them in my hair, cups my face, and I'm leaning down, breathing him in, his eyes start to close and we press our bodies together so I can feel every inch of him. But then he stops and the air between us changes. It's cold now.

I know and so I wait.

Of course.

Poppy.

I press my forehead into his chest and sigh. "I know," I say.

He folds me into a hug and I fall back onto the bed. The feeling of excitement fades into longing.

I feel him breathing and his heart is pounding beneath my cheek and his arms are tight around me. I expect him to let go, get up, leave now that we've stepped back into reality, but he doesn't. He stays exactly here.

"Virginia," he says, and I love the sound of my name in his mouth. "We can't."

"I know," I say again.

"But I want to stay."

I pull back and look at him. Right now I love everything about him. His face, his body, his identity, his soul.

His eyes pour back into mine. "I really want to stay."

"Okay," I say.

I rest my hand close beneath his chin.

I can still feel his heartbeat, steady as a metronome.

It gets to be a long time between sentences.

"I think I'll always be a little bit sad," I say.

He rolls toward me, hands in my hair.

"It's like a condition of my life," I say.

His eyes are closed like he's falling asleep.

"Do you feel like there's a theme? Like, a theme to your life?" I say.

"I guess I would say guilt," Rumi says.

The stars keep spinning around the earth. I imagine them streaking by, leaving streamers of light in their wake.

When the sky turns from black to less black to gray I sit up and look at Rumi. I'm not going to be able to sleep, I think. His face is relaxed, eyes closed, throat exposed and bristly with nighttime growth. His shirt rides up and his shorts are low and I can see the hollow of his hip, smooth and purple with shadow.

I feel such a strong urge to dip my fingers beneath his waistband and to touch the part of him that I can't see. My heart races just thinking about it.

His eyes open like he's startled and he reaches for me and I go to him, lying my cheek on his chest, on the soft cotton of his shirt. He's not awake, not really. It's like he needs me, the way he holds me and tangles his hands into my hair. And he kisses me just above my ear and then he presses his face into my neck and I lie there feeling like he is holding all of me, my whole entire self.

We stand in my morning-cold kitchen, filled with watery sunlight. I don't want to let the air in between us. I make coffee. I drink it black and Rumi calls it puddle water. We sit close to the window so the sun is warm on my face.

"I think it's okay," Rumi says. "It's just one night, and we didn't actually do anything."

We didn't do anything. We didn't kiss. We didn't have sex. We didn't break any rules. Except we did. I stare into my coffee until I feel his hand on my hair, pushing it back, tucking it behind my ear.

"Last night was beautiful, but we can't do it again," he says.

I nod. It's all I can manage.

"I have to work," he says at the door. He lingers in the sun of the stoop and looks at my face in the shadows of my house. He touches my wrist.

"You have to go to work," I remind him.

"Right. Work." But still he doesn't leave. "Virginia," he says, and he pulls me into his arms, his hand on the back of my neck through my tangled hair and every part of my body is touching every part of his body for a sweet powerful moment and then he does leave.

Eight

I WALK LYRA out after tutoring. She runs and jumps as soon as she's out the door and tries to kick her heels together mid-jump and then falls, catching herself with her elbows and hands. I jog to catch up. She holds up her palms and I take them. They're scraped and bleeding and her skin is smooth and hot.

"Are you okay?" I think she's trying not to cry, like she has to be tough. Watching her try not to cry, I feel like crying for her even though it's not a big deal, even though it's just a scrape.

"I'm fine," she says.

I sit next to her and she presses her scraped hands to her legs. I hum in sympathy and try to think of something to say. "Any more midnight movie adventures?"

"No, but I did a little fire outside, like I made a little mini fire and cooked marshmallows. It was late. I think it was like three." She inspects her scrapes and then presses them back into her legs. Then she says, "Did you ever sneak out?"

I nod. "Yeah. I snuck out a lot. My parents didn't really care, though."

"I don't even have parents," Lyra says. "So where did you go?"

"I would just wander. I went to the library or the community center and then they closed for the night and then I don't know."

Sometimes it was okay. On warm clear nights I could sit awhile and look up or out or somewhere beautiful. But then the feeling of adventure faded and I was just a kid alone outside and it was late. On the cold nights when it rained there was never anywhere dry enough. All I wanted to do was find somewhere safe to sleep.

"But was it fun?" she says.

And I say, "No. Not really."

"I have this friend."

I nod, waiting.

"He might meet me sometime, he says. For ice cream or something."

"Who is this friend?" I say.

Lyra shrugs and looks the other way. Her cheek ripens with a smile I can't see.

"Is your friend, like, a boyfriend?" I ask.

She shrugs again.

Rumi's yellow Volvo chugs around the corner. He pulls up to the curb and I watch as he realizes that Lyra is hurt. His face changes. It mirrors her pain. Then he smooths it out. Calm, just calm. "What happened?" he asks.

She holds up her hands and he kisses her scrapes and presses her hands to his cheeks. She pulls away with a little scoff. "I'm fine," she says, and this time she seems to mean it. "Can I play soccer for a little?" she asks.

"Sure, grab your ball," he says to Lyra. And she runs off while Rumi parks.

I wait even though I don't know what I'm waiting for. I think he takes extra time watching Lyra and his hands are in his pockets and I know I should leave and I know he should only just say hi but we keep standing there. And then he's striding toward me and I meet him on the sidewalk. He pulls me into his arms and hugs me so tight and I press my face into his neck. And I don't even know what we're doing or how I could explain this or make it even kind of okay and not like I'm betraying my best forever friend. I just know I feel like I need him. I just know I really want to be here with him.

We move to the shade of a magnolia tree and watch Lyra kick a ball around the field and we smoke a joint Rumi pulled out of his back pocket.

"So you smoke weed but you don't drink," I say.

Rumi nods.

I knock my heels together. "How come?"

"My mom drank a lot. She had a stroke when I was fifteen."

I stare at my feet.

"She's dead."

I want to keep staring but I look him in the eye. "I remember hearing about that. I'm so sorry."

"When people say that, I always feel this urge to respond with 'It's okay,' you know, to reassure them or something." He watches Lyra charging around the field, arms up, bellowing. "But it's not okay."

He closes his eyes and pinches the bridge of his nose like he has a headache. I press my forehead against his shoulder. I find his hand with both of mine. I hold it, tight and warm. "What about your dad?"

"My dad's an asshole. I haven't seen him in years. Otherwise we'd be in Montana. He's been there since I was a kid."

"I'm glad you're here. I'm so glad. I would miss you."

"You wouldn't even know me," he says.

"I would still miss you."

I ride with Rumi to take Lyra home and Ro texts and I remember I'm supposed to meet her new person, like ten minutes ago. I look at Rumi and he shrugs and that settles that I guess.

im sorry! omw, I text back.

I'm an alligator, she texts me.

what

I'm a mamapapa coming for you, Ro responds.

why are you so weird

its david bowie you postulant

She's pacing in front of the restaurant when we pull up. "Ma!" she says into her phone, rolling her eyes at me. "I know! Yes, I will I know goodbyeIloveyou." She sees Rumi. "Hello, where did you come from?"

"Well, when a mommy and a daddy love each other very much . . ." Rumi starts.

Ro grimaces and says, "Gross," and I know she notices when Rumi bumps my shoulder with his shoulder and I smile because I can't help it.

Hannah has red hair and pretty pale skin. She shares bites of her poke with me because I got tuna and cilantro and she got salmon and wasabi and she laughs when I admit that hers is better. Ro smiles at the two of us laughing together and then glances at Rumi, who is absorbed in his brown rice and shrimp, unaware that this is weird.

"So what's Suzanna yelling at you about?" I say to Ro.

She rolls her eyes again and finishes chewing. "She's mad because I was hanging out with Hannah and forgot to take the dog to the groomer."

"We should just give Rita May a bath ourselves," Hannah says.

"Really?" Ro says.

"Yeah, it'll be fun."

"Have you met Rita May?" I say.

"She's massive," Hannah says, and shrugs.

"Ro's dad says she's part mastiff, part grizzly bear."

"And possibly part stegosaurus because her brain is so teeny," Ro says, and laughs.

"Rita May is the best. You guys need to shut up," Hannah says.

Ro leans across the table and kisses her sweetly and I look at Rumi, who's smiling.

Ro keeps looking at me like, *We need to talk*, and finally when I say I have to go to the bathroom she follows me saying "Pee party!" and laughing but I know she is ready to pounce.

"Virginia," she says. She twists a braid around her topknot but her eyes are on me in the mirror.

"What?"

She sits on the stool in the corner and says, "Just tell me."

"It's nothing."

"It's not nothing. You guys, like, crackle with electricity."

"Nothing's happened!"

"But do you want it to?"

I lean against the wall and press my fingers into my forehead. "What the fuck am I doing, Ro?"

"I don't know."

I pull down my pants and sit on the toilet.

"But also—" Ro says, then stops.

"But what?"

"This might be a really shitty thing to say," Ro says.

"I love shitty things."

"Well, I mean, where even is Poppy? Have you heard from her? Has Rumi?"

I shake my head. "I've texted her every single day."

"Right," Ro says. "I'm not saying it's all fine. I'm just saying that she like surgically removed herself from this situation and that has to mean something, right?"

But I shrug because I have no idea.

"Hannah is beautiful," I say.

"She's going to Stanford next year."

"Are you in love?"

Ro laughs. "Not quite." Then she closes her eyes. "But maybe soon."

"Oh em gee!" I say.

When I'm done washing my hands Ro says, "I won't say anything." She stands up and I wrap my arms around her waist and squeeze and she hugs me back and we stand there, embracing in the bathroom like weirdos.

Rumi and Hannah are playing tic-tac-toe on a napkin as we walk up.

As Rumi and me drive away, I feel a rush of love for Ro. *love you*, I text her.

She texts me back right away: *je t'aime aussi.*

Sometimes they talk about stuff. My parents. Sometimes they talk about Him my-dad's-friend-who-probably-tried-to-get-in-my-room-last-time.

Like it's no big deal.

"Is He coming tonight though?" my mom says.

"I don't know," my dad says back.

"But if He is I need to go to the store."

"I know, but I don't know."

"Just find out. I need to make sure we have enough to eat." She keeps going, needling my dad even though he's getting annoyed.

I am small in the corner waiting for them to leave.

He pulls out his phone, keys in his other hand, coffee in a travel mug on the counter. "Yo, you showing up tonight?"

He spins his keys around one finger.

She clacks her nails, waiting for the answer: Is He coming, yes or no.

"Right." My dad looks at my mom and nods and then heads to the garage. She clops out the front door.

I turn to the cupboard and find my mug. My Thalia mug.

The ceramic is warm in my hands as I head to the front

stoop to watch the yardwork and kid playing and as I cross the threshold the mug tumbles out of my hand. Rolling in the air, spinning at the center of a fountain of coffee. It hits the cement and shatters into four or five big pieces and a million little ones, splattering out in a concentric circle like a still-art firework.

My hands are still shaking as I text Thalia: *are your parents out tonight?* I just want to see her. I just want it to be okay. I feel like the mug is our friendship and I just broke it.

My phone buzzes in my hand but it's not Thalia, it's Edison again. I delete the message and wait.

Just my dad, comes the reply.

want to hang out?

Paz is at that PFLAG conference and Ro's with that new girl tonight, she texts me back.

I turn my phone over and over in my hands. I'm not sure if I should keep trying, or if Thalia just wants me to give up and leave her alone.

I'm probably just hanging out with Edison, she texts before I respond.

Edison texts me again. Again I delete it.

I want Rumi to text so badly. And he does.

I want him to and when I feel my pocket vibrate and pull out my phone I know it's him.

watcha doin

hi, I text him back.

I know I need to leave and I know I can't come back. Rumi said whenever, just whenever.

I text Rumi again. And then I run.

I get to where the road dissolves into an empty lot, gravel and grass, quiet and green, and there is nothing but blackberry thorns and rabbits, and I stop. My whole body is throbbing with hot blood.

It isn't long before I hear the crunch of tires slowing down and then a door slams and then he's standing next to me.

"Hi," Rumi says. "Did you run all the way from your house?"

I nod and wipe sweat from my brow. "Thanks for meeting me."

There is something earnest about him, standing there in his tan shorts and white T-shirt and high-tops. His hands in his pockets. I am going to ask him if I can stay at his house tonight and I'm nervous about it.

I have to do it. There's no question about that. I'm just not sure how to get there.

"Hang out with me? I need to sit and breathe."

"Do you run a lot?" Rumi sits down on the grass.

I sit next to him. I feel the wind between our bodies. "I try."

"You must if you can run so far." He looks over his shoulder in the direction of my house.

"It's farther than I normally run, but it felt really necessary, I guess, so I kept running."

"What do you mean, necessary?"

"Not sure. Like I'm atoning."

He doesn't say anything, so I keep going. "Like pushing my body so hard, it's my penance."

"For what?"

"For having a body. For doing shitty things with it."

"What kinds of things?"

I roll my eyes. "You know."

"No. I don't."

"He keeps texting me. Edison. And I just don't know how to tell him no. Tell him to fuck off."

"He's such a piece of shit," Rumi says.

"But it's like I am too, so what can I really say?"

Rumi laughs like he can't believe it. "Edison is a piece of shit because he pressures you into sex and doesn't give a fuck who he hurts. He values his orgasm over all this, like, destruction he leaves in his wake. I can't tell you why you struggle with telling him no but I do know *that* doesn't make you like Edison."

"But I mean why is it so hard? It's just one word."

Rumi doesn't say anything.

"Also I just like, I want sex to feel good. I mean not just physically but emotionally. I don't want to feel like I'm performing a service. I don't want to feel like I'm just meeting somebody else's need. I don't want to feel like I'm just a hole to masturbate into." I draw in a shuddering breath.

Rumi tilts his head, his eyes on me, a deep crease between his brows.

"I want to be something more, something different than just fuckable." I say the thing from the deepest part of my heart. The hardest thing to say. "I want to be loved." I close my eyes. I can't look at him.

"Virginia."

But I keep my eyes closed.

"Virginia." He doesn't touch me, but I feel his words on my skin. "I love your good heart."

It's the most beautiful thing anybody has ever said to me.

I'm just . . . I'm not pretending anymore.

Nine

IT TURNS OUT I don't have to ask him. He invites me. The sun is going down when we get there. The shadows are long and edged with golden light. Lyra runs through the orchard with Trunks, her shadow flashing between trees. Rumi holds my hand as we go up the stairs into the rickety old house, painted white and glowing like a diamond in the reflected sunset.

Rumi squeezes my hand and pushes open the screen door with a long groaning creak. There are shafts of sunlight here and there filled with swirling dust. There are chimes singing in the background, and below that the steady crackling intonation of news radio.

"Want to see my room?" Rumi says.

It's an attic room and the clapboard walls are thin and it's really hot in here, but he has fans in every window. There are paisley patterned sheets pinned over his windows and they billow in the breeze and flashes of light break against his walls. He has a mattress on the floor made up with bohemian sheets and thin blankets. The picture of me at the beach, smiling up into the sky, is tacked to the wall by his bed.

. . .

In the quiet of his nighttime room we lie in his bed, our legs tangled together. His window is open and the wind is delicious tumbling in, delicious and cool and wet. Rumi wraps his arms around me and presses in behind me. His hand is right below my breasts and I can feel it, something in the tension of his arm, how he wants to touch me there but he doesn't. I press my head back against his shoulder and he tightens his arms and buries his face in my naked neck, his lips on my bare skin. A hot shock runs through my body, in my chest, in my belly, in between my legs, and suddenly it's hard to breathe and I have goose bumps all over my arms.

He scoots back away from me. "Sorry," he says, and I turn over to face him. His cheeks are flushed in the dim yellow lamp light. He opens his mouth to say something and then closes it again and I can tell he's embarrassed but I don't know why and then I notice. He's hard under his shorts.

"Rumi," I say. We can't we can't we can't. But I want to. But we can't. But god, I want to. Like he has his own personal gravity I'm leaning in, pulling him toward me like I have to answer his gravity with mine, I can feel his heat, I can feel his body, pressing into me, he's doing it too, it's not just me, it's not just him, it's both of us. Kiss me. Now. Do it. I'm ready. Kiss me kiss me kiss me.

But I don't, we don't, because somebody pounds on the door. "Rumi?" It's Lyra. "I had a bad dream."

He jolts like he's been electrocuted. "Fuck off!" he barks, his hands tight on my arms like he wants to stop me from pulling away.

I close my eyes. I can feel my cheeks burning.

"Fuck," Rumi says, quiet. "I'm such an asshole. I should go check on her."

I press my hands onto my face. I'm cold without him. We didn't even kiss. He comes back in. "I'm sorry," he says. When I don't respond Rumi curls into me, gathering my limbs into his arms and legs, and presses his face into my neck and holds me so tight that somehow I feel okay again.

In that moment I love him.

After we've slept for a while, he gets up to turn off his lamp. I watch him as he lingers at the window, looking out over the rows and rows of trees that look like bones in the moonlight. When he comes back to bed I turn toward him and he touches my face. My cheekbone. My chin.

Rumi makes me a spinach and tomato omelet for breakfast. He slices an avocado and arranges it across the top. I smile as he sprinkles cilantro and salt, wiggling his fingers with a flourish.

"God," I say through the mouthful.

"Good?" He smiles and sits down across from me, taking a bite from the other end.

"How are you this good of a cook? Aren't teenage boys supposed to be focused on nothing but sex?"

He laughs. "Well."

I realize what I said and I'm pretty sure I'm blushing like some kind of debutant.

After breakfast, Lyra is sitting on the stairs outside throwing a ball for Trunks.

"Can I?" I sit next to her. She hands me the tennis ball, slimy with dog spit, and I hurl it into the peach trees. I think of the way Rumi ran to her after tutoring, when he saw that she was hurt.

Trunks comes tearing out of the trees, the ball wedged between his teeth, and Lyra leaps up to meet him. She skids on her knees in the mud and wraps her arms around his neck, pushing her face into his. She sits down next to me again and puts her head on my shoulder. I think about putting my arm around her but I don't move and then I obey the urge and I do. I wrap my arm around her shoulder, lightly, barely, like she is skittish and she might bolt. Her pants are frayed and wet and brown and green with mud and moss and she's barefoot, wiggling her toes. She jerks her head up like she's suddenly self-conscious and throws the ball again. "My aunt says if I don't get him trained I have to get rid of him. Did you know I didn't ask if I could have him?" She laughs loud like it's hilarious, then stops. "He chewed up her shoe and also part of the carpet. And also he dug up Firefly's leeks, so now we have to chicken-wire all the plots."

"Who's Firefly?" I say.

"It's, like, his nickname." She flaps her hand at an older man in a paisley shirt, working in the dahlias. Trunks spits the ball out at our feet. "Anyway, the neighbors gave Trunks to me. They said they couldn't keep him because he kept eating stuff and chewing stuff up, so they gave him to me and I took him home. Rumi was so mad." She laughs again. It's like she can't help it.

The screen door opens and closes and I feel Rumi behind me. His sits down with one leg on either side of me and I lean back against his chest with his arms on my knees, his chin on my shoulder. "I can feel you blinking," I say. "Now I can feel you smile."

He laughs and almost but not quite kisses me, right next to my mouth.

We take Trunks for a walk, all of us. He yanks along on his leash and I try to let Lyra get ahead of us. Rumi slows down next to me. I can feel it, that he also wants to be alone. But then Lyra notices we're lagging behind her and she waits for us, saying, "Come on, slowpokes! My clothes are going out of style here!"

I roll my eyes because she stole that line from *The Sandlot*. Rumi glances at me. He can tell I'm annoyed. "Want to play my Switch when we get home?" he asks her.

"Really? You'll let me?" She grins big and says to me, "He never lets me play his Switch!"

She runs ahead of us, Trunks racing alongside, and Rumi threads his fingers through mine. I feel electric. I feel hot in my hand and the side that is closest to him. I feel everything, everything, in the space between us.

But he frowns after her. And when we get back to their house and he hands her his Switch, his smile drops off his face as soon as she's not looking. It's almost like he feels guilty for getting rid of her even though it seems okay to me for a seventeen-year-old to not always want to hang out with his eleven-year-old sister especially when he's hanging out with a girl he hopefully kind of likes.

"Doesn't she have any friends?" I say when we disappear into his room.

Rumi shrugs. "She used to go over to Chihiro's house all the time, but she hasn't in a while."

"Did you ever invite any of her friends over here?" I ask.

He gives me a blank look. "No," he says. "What am I going to do with a bunch of eleven-year-old girls?"

"What about your aunt?"

"She's just really busy. I mean she tries, but she works nights and, you know."

"It just seems unfair to me," I say.

"What?"

"Just the whole thing. You're not her parent."

Rumi pulls me into the crook of his arm, hand warm and heavy on my hair, and I close my eyes. "Never mind," he says, but not like he means forget it, like he means let's not worry about it right now because I'm here and you're here and let's just enjoy this moment we have together.

I imagine his hands on either side of my face. I imagine our kiss starting out sweet and light and then becoming deeper and deeper and deeper until I'm gasping for breath. Wrapping my arms around his neck and the feeling in the space between us as he leans into me and I cradle him with my arms and lips and thighs and hips. And the light around us ebbs away into the starry night beneath my eyelids.

I imagine lying in bed with him and moments occur to me in bright warm flashes. Him on top of me, breathing into my neck, my legs wrapped around his hips. I might cry after the first time because it is so beautiful and good, and because when I'm with him *I* will feel beautiful and good.

And he'll hold me while I cry and tell me he loves me and that I am safe with him.

Ten

THALIA AND ME look alike. We always have ever since we were little. Dishwater blond, thin, peachy pale skin, regular features. But Thalia wore coordinating outfits. Her hair was nicely brushed. Put together. Clean. Pretty. Somebody paid attention to the way Thalia looked. Somebody dressed her up like a doll and made her pretty. I'm sure I didn't look cared for. I'm sure my neglect was apparent if anybody really looked.

Once upon a time when we were in second grade some boys were harassing Paz. They called her a chick-with-a-dick and a fag. She transitioned in first grade, started using the girls' bathroom and she/her pronouns. We were at recess and the teachers weren't paying attention. Paz looked like she was trying really hard not to care, but her bottom lip was trembling and her cheeks were flushed. I couldn't tell if she was about to get really mad and throw rocks at them or cry. Probably both.

Paz and I had been friends since kindergarten and I wanted to defend Paz. I was trying to work up the courage to yell at the boys. To condemn their bigotry with big words. To so eloquently defend Paz's right to life, liberty, and the pursuit of happiness that they would instantly fling themselves at her feet and beg for forgiveness and repent their evil intolerant ways. I'm pretty sure I was thinking more about myself and how brave I would be to defend Paz than actually defending Paz.

While I was busy imagining my act of gallantry, Thalia ran up behind the boys and pantsed Edison. (Of course he was one of them.) Which made him cry and everybody else laugh except Paz. She still looked ready to cry. Thalia took her hand and led her to a teacher. Edison and the other boys got suspended and we had an assembly on tolerance.

That was the first year I wanted to be friends with Thalia. It wasn't until third grade that I decided she wasn't too good for me. During the social chaos of a field trip to the Woodland Park Zoo we bonded over the baby pandas. Paz was sick that day.

That day, Thalia and me were friends.

Every year she got to invite one friend along on her birthday trip with her dad. Thalia's mom always stayed home. Mount St. Helens, Victoria, Portland, Lake Chelan. Somewhere beautiful, cool, unique. She invited Paz second grade, third grade, fourth grade. She invited me fifth grade. We went to Santa Fe. On the long dusty drive I stared out the window at the red arches and cactuses and thought about Paz. I wondered if it meant something that Thalia chose me instead of Paz. I thought about Paz, sitting at home. I wondered if she was sad or angry or maybe she didn't care that this year she was left behind.

They stopped going after that. That was the last birthday trip.

I remember the road on that trip. Bright blue sky and bright red rock. It baked with dry heat and cooked me from the inside out until I thought all my veins ran with dust instead of blood. Thalia's dad drove, singing songs and fiddling with the radio, changing stations to fit his mood. We stopped at burger stands and taco trucks, anything that he considered independent, nothing too corporate. I remember pulling into the hotel the first night. Swimming in the over-chlorinated pool. Eating microwave popcorn and watching whatever movie was on HBO. I remember thinking it was weird that he got me my own room. That I wasn't sharing with Thalia. I was scared of sleeping alone in that big cold room. Scared of monsters. Scared of beasts.

I'm pulled out of my reverie when Rumi flops down next to me. We're swimming at a little strip of grassy beach at Green Lake. Thalia and Paz and Langston and Ro and Hannah splash in the water, reflecting white, bright in my eyes. I watch them and smile and turn to Rumi.

"You should teach me to run," he says.

I laugh.

"No seriously, I want to learn. I want to go running with you."

I imagine running next to him, our strong limbs pumping, tall grass whipping our legs. I rearrange my bag, punching it into shape, and lie down with my head on it like a pillow. Rumi pulls my bare legs into his lap. I love the feel of my skin on his skin. I close my eyes. The sun is red through my eyelids.

I think I fall asleep for a minute. I don't mean to. It's just so hard to sleep at home. I'm so tired. I jolt when I hear Thalia's voice and I feel her sit down next to me. I open my eyes and sit up but not quickly enough. She's looking as I slide my legs off Rumi's lap, as he removes his hands from my naked skin. Ro and Paz arrange themselves on the blanket. Langston drinks from his water bottle. Hannah asks for the sunscreen and starts reapplying.

"So what about Medusa," I say, blathering, nervous and trying to cover it up. "For our senior project? She's a really interesting example of a figure in mythology with a lot of power. I mean, people have been telling her story for thousands of years. And also it's interesting that she gets punished for having sex, you know?"

Thalia just looks at me. For so long Ro and Paz and Hannah and even Rumi go quiet and watch. Her expression gets darker and darker and finally she says, "First of all, Medusa was raped. She didn't decide to fuck around like some people do."

Ro looks at Hannah and Paz looks down at her hands and Langston and Rumi are looking at me. I can feel Rumi's eyes on my hot red cheeks.

"And honestly, I don't think this is working. I want to do my senior project on something else. I don't feel like we have similar work styles or whatever."

"Oh, okay, I mean, that makes sense," I start to say, and then I feel a strong and infuriating urge to cry. I can't cry here. I can't. I stand up and Rumi stands up too, next to me, close to my body, and Thalia's eyes widen and then she's also standing. When Rumi takes my hand all Thalia sees is sex. Even though that's not what it is. Even though I don't even know what it is.

"You fucking slut," she says.

"Thalia!" Ro says. "What the hell?"

"Are you kidding? She's such a whore!" Thalia turns to me, shaking with anger. "You don't give a fuck who you hurt, do you? Not even Poppy matters to you! Don't pretend like this thing with Rumi isn't the exact same thing you always do."

Paz looks like she wants to cry. Langston is looking at me and shaking his head like he agrees with Thalia. Everybody else is just staring.

It's funny how something can be so devastating and so quiet at the same time. If somebody were looking down from a helicopter this would seem like nothing. They would think we were just a bunch of teenagers hanging out, having fun.

And that's it. I don't say anything because it's all true. I don't defend myself because I can't. I just stand there until Rumi tugs on my hand and pulls me away and I can hear voices behind me but I have no idea what they're saying.

We're next to his car and I stand shuddering in Rumi's arms with my face in his chest, my eyes burning. The shadows grow and stretch. The sun is still hot but most of the beach is shady and cold and people start to leave. There are goose bumps on Rumi's naked skin.

Ro brings me my things and hugs me and whispers, "It's going to be okay," and leaves with Hannah, their interlinked hands swinging between them. I don't see Paz or Thalia, we just get in the car. It's warm and humid inside like a small summer just for us. I am tired and my skin is sticky with sunscreen and sand and I sit on a towel in the passenger seat.

On the way home I realize it. Rumi didn't defend me. I didn't defend myself but Rumi didn't defend me either. He didn't say anything. Even though this is about him too. He's been here with me the whole time.

It starts to rain as we sit in traffic. Red brake lights flash in his face. A raindrop slides down the windshield and the shadow of it slides down Rumi's face like a tear.

Eleven

IT'S FINE. I run out the front door without saying goodbye to my parents, who are sitting in silence staring at their phones with the TV deafening. I brought an extra set of clothes because maybe just maybe somebody will let me spend the night.

It's fine it's fine it's fine.

Thalia might not even be there and even if she is, what, is she like never going to talk to me again? Nothing even happened with Rumi, not really.

It's fine.

I run to Ro's house because she's driving. Noah, her dad, lets me in. He's tall and thin and he has a baby face and great big anime eyes and a gentle way of acting. I think he's the only adult man who doesn't make me nervous. "Hi Virginia," he says, and I can already see the dad questions forming behind his eyes. "How's your summer going? Got a job?"

"I'm doing some tutoring at the community center," I say, edging in the door.

Suzanna is pacing around in the kitchen. She's arguing with somebody on the phone. "But she said she would go on the record," she says. "I'm going to keep working on this. Yes. Yes, that's exactly what I'm saying. I've got three women willing to be quoted. I've got two sources from inside the campus police and one from the office of the Title Nine coordinator."

Noah shuts the door behind me. "Her editor," he says. "Want something to drink? A snack? I just made Ro a PB and J with the new huckleberry jam Suzanna made. It's got jalapeno in it this time."

"The sandwich?" I say.

"The jelly. It's really good. Want to try it?"

Suzanna says, "Don't tell me this is about standards. I've met the standards—no, I've exceeded the standards." And then she goes out onto the back porch and closes the door behind her and I can't hear her anymore and I turn back to Noah.

"That's okay. I'm not hungry. Is Ro upstairs?"

"What are you going to tell people about Rumi?" Ro says as soon as I get to her room. She's got a half-eaten sandwich in her hand.

"Hello," I say.

She yanks her shirt up with one hand and gets it stuck over her head. "Take this," she says, waving the sandwich around.

I try a bite. "I wouldn't know what to say." It's good, spicy and sweet and salty. "Good jelly," I say.

"What do you mean?" Ro says, tying her bikini around her ribs. "Can you help me?"

"I don't even know what's happening between us. We're not together, like that. We just hang out a lot." I knot the strings behind her back.

She gives me a skeptical look.

"I'm afraid," I say.

"Of what?"

"Of what people will think. Of how Poppy will feel. If she ever picks up the phone."

Ro nods.

"I might be a little in love with him," I say.

"Just a little?"

"Just the tip."

"Well, it doesn't count if it's just the tip."

"How's Hannah?" I ask.

Ro frowns and starts shoving things into her pool bag. She doesn't say anything.

"What?" I say.

She shakes her head.

"Oh my god, you're killing me. What? What's going on?"

"We're kind of having a thing. We need to go, though, she's waiting for us."

I look at Ro while we're driving, frowning at her hands on the steering wheel. She doesn't look like her normal self. She looks diminished.

Hannah is waiting outside when we get to the pool, smiling and waving, but Ro doesn't acknowledge her until we're parked and out of the car. Ro's bare arm tightens around her bag and even though it's hot I watch as a stripe of goose bumps erupts along her skin. She's frowning at her feet. I link my arm through hers, tight and close.

"Hey!" Hannah says.

"Hey." Ro meets her eyes but doesn't smile.

It's all so awkward. And it's worse because I know Ro is hurting but I don't know why. The pool water is cold and clear and for a while I float in it, with my ears submerged so I can't hear anything. Floating with my eyes closed, it's like there's nothing. Nothing anywhere. But then I get too cold. My skin is pruned and prickled. Ro hands me her towel, which is bigger and fluffier than mine, and I wrap myself in it and lie on the chair next to her and Hannah and I can tell their energy is still off. They haven't worked it out yet, whatever it is.

Hannah is trying to get close to Ro, putting her hand on Ro's leg, leaning her head on Ro's shoulder, trying to feed Ro tiny mandarin wedges, but Ro isn't letting her. Hannah tries again and Ro says, "No, I'm sorry, but I don't want to be touched by you right now."

Hannah jerks her head back like she's been slapped. Her skin turns red and blotchy. She doesn't say anything. She just looks injured.

I look at Ro and Ro looks back at me, obviously upset, embarrassed. *Love you*, I mouth. Ro turns to Hannah and says, "You're not being fair."

"*I'm* not being fair?" Hannah says back.

"No, you're not. It's not fair for you to expect me to be just totally okay with your decision not to tell your parents about me."

I lean back in the chair and close my eyes, trying to give them a little bit of privacy, but I reach for Ro's hand. She clasps it tight next to her thigh.

"Ro, I'm sorry," Hannah says through my closed eyes. She

sounds like she's holding back tears. "I am. I'm just not ready."

Ro's hand tightens on mine and then she releases it and I peek at her. She is sitting up, leaning toward Hannah. Hannah has one hand on either cheek, staring at Ro, and her eyes are shimmering with held back tears. "You don't have to be ready. You don't have to do anything. But whatever you do or don't do, it does affect me and my feelings and I can't control that. I don't want to be touched by somebody who is keeping me a secret. It makes me feel gross."

Hannah covers her eyes with one hand and then gets up and walks away, toward the bathrooms.

I sit up now and put my arms around Ro, pulling her back against me. "What's going on?" I say.

"Her parents don't know she's gay."

"Are they conservative or something?"

"No, that's not it. She's their only child. I think they have her whole life planned out. They have all these ideas about who she's supposed to be."

I nod.

"She's afraid of telling them."

"Keep talking," I say. I'm not sure what her feelings are and I want to draw them out rather than make assumptions.

"Her parents think she'll get married and have kids."

"Being gay doesn't stop her from doing those things."

"Virginia, when they're imagining their future grandkids they're not imagining Hannah adopting them with a Black woman."

"Okay, but is that what you even want? I mean, you're seventeen."

"No, I know. I just . . ." She sighs and rubs her eyes like she's tired. "I feel like she's hiding me. Like she's hiding the fact that I'm a girl and that I'm Black."

"Why do you think she's hiding that you're Black?" I ask. "Did something happen?"

"I can tell her parents are uncomfortable around me. And that made Hannah uncomfortable. And now she won't tell them that we're together," Ro says.

I wrap my arm around her shoulders, warm from the sun and soft and fragrant from sunscreen and lotion, and she leans her head against mine.

"I don't want to be hidden. It makes me feel ashamed. That she is ashamed of me makes me feel ashamed of myself. My skin, my sexuality, my whole self."

"I'm sorry. I love you. I love your whole self. Everything about you is lovely and amazing."

"I love you too," Ro says.

"Do you trust her? To be forthcoming with you? To be good to you?"

She shrugs. "I don't know. I mean, I really like her. Like a lot. She is super cool. She's smart. She's beautiful. She's kind. But this sucks."

"What are you going to do?"

"Nothing right now. I want to think about it. I want to talk to my mom and dad about it."

I squint at her with the sun hot on my face. "You're so healthy."

"I'm trying to be. C'est la vie." She tucks a damp strand of hair behind my ear and shrugs. "I'm going to go find her," Ro says. She packs up Hannah's stuff with hers. "Can you take the bus? Or get a ride with Paz and Thalia whenever they show up?"

"I'll be fine. Go. Love you."

"No you," she says.

"You."

"Me," Ro says, and laughs as she's leaving.

Thalia and Paz appear in a tumble of tanned limbs, telling inside jokes that somehow I feel left out of even though I was probably there when they began. I try not to hunch my shoulders. Somehow it takes all of my skinny courage to stand up and walk toward them.

Paz sees me and waves, her face open and friendly. But then Thalia shakes her head at Paz and I can hear Thalia's low angry voice but not the words she's saying. Finally Paz gives me an upset look and I just say fuck it and leave.

"Virginia!" Paz chases me outside. "Wait."

I bite the inside of my cheek. I don't want her to see me cry.

"Don't be sad," she implores me. "Thalia is just going through stuff right now."

"She's been acting pissed at me for like weeks, Paz, and it's just getting worse."

Paz looks down, smoothing her hands over her tie-dyed swim skirt.

"And the worst part is," I say, my voice breaking as I ignore the unspoken territory of me-and-Edison, "I'm not even doing anything. And she's getting more and more shitty with me."

"But Rumi." Paz squints at me. "I mean, it seems like something is going on with him."

"But it's not. We haven't even kissed."

Her surprise hurts more than anything else.

"Do you believe me?" I say.

"Yes Virginia, of course I believe you." She reaches for my hand and I let her take it. Paz pulls me into a hug and I lean my head against her shoulder. She smells like sunscreen and lemon and powdered sugar and I sag into her, letting her hold up the weight of all the feelings, all the shame that has been coming on for years even though I've been trying to ignore it.

When I straighten up she keeps hold of my hand. "I think it's going to be okay. Like, all of it. I think it's all going to be okay. You just need to talk to Poppy. And you should talk to Thalia too, you know, eventually. You just need to give her some space to get through some shit right now. I think you guys will be okay. I think you will be okay. Okay? Virginia?"

I nod.

"God, I'm rambling. I'm going to go back in. Text me, okay?"

I nod again and Paz runs back to lie beside Thalia and try to convince her to not hate me, probably.

Twelve

I FORGOT MY headphones. I walk down the hill to tutoring, my legs straining and my heels skidding. I regret it when a car full of dudes rushes by, screaming and honking. I keep walking and their cacophony fades and it's quiet again and I swing in the direction of Langston's house thinking maybe I can ride with him. But when I see him thunking his bulging leather shoulder bag into the passenger seat of his car looking like an old man professor with a stack of books, I feel a hot pulse of shame and anger, somehow. Thinking about the way Thalia rejected me at the pool. Thinking about the things she said to me at the beach and the way Langston shook his head at me. Like he agreed.

He looks up at me. "Want a ride?" He smiles, but I can't smile back. His face changes and I think he can tell I'm spoiling for a fight. When he turns to his car I follow him.

"Don't you have something you want to say?"

He crosses his arms over his chest. "I'm not sure anything I have to say would be productive."

"Why do you always say that? Even when we were ten and fighting over Legos you were like, *this isn't productive.*" I imitate his sanctimonious ten-year-old voice, feeling mean.

"I don't know, maybe because I'm a functional human?" he snaps back at me.

"So, like, I'm such a slut anyway that there's no way I'll ever recover?"

"No, Virginia." Langston frowns at me. "I don't even use that word."

"You can still think it of me. It's like you and Thalia and Paz and everybody think that there is something fundamentally morally wrong with a girl having sex. When I'm not in a relationship or we're not in love or I'm only fourteen or fifteen or sixteen."

"That's not it," Langston says. "It's not that you have sex. It's that you're doing it with your friend's boyfriend."

"But I'm not! And anyway, it wasn't all my fault."

"That's not what I'm saying! You're just, like, assuming I think it's your fault."

"You don't even know! You don't know what it's like. There's so much pressure, to please, to comply, to go with the flow, to be cool and chill and go along with whatever some dude wants of you. Ask Paz if you don't know!"

"Leave Paz out of this," he snaps.

"Let's call her!"

"Virginia," Langston says, but I'm already dialing.

Paz picks up, her voice full of tears.

"What? What's wrong?" All my anger is gone.

Langston rubs the back of his neck, looking down.

"It's Langston," Paz says. "He said he wants to go to Williams."

"Williams?"

"It's on the East Coast!" Paz wails.

"So like . . ." I say, then pause, looking at Langston for help, but he won't look at me.

"He said he's going to apply early decision, which means if he gets in he *has* to go and he'll definitely get in, which means he'll definitely go and that means we'll definitely break up and I don't want to break up!"

"Paz," I say.

"What?"

"This is like months away. You're catastrophizing."

"He's a shitty shoebox," Paz says, sniffling.

"He's not a shitty shoebox."

Langston looks like he's going to laugh and meets my eyes and then reaches for the phone. I hand it to him and he walks away and I hear him murmuring to Paz, so soothing, so sweet. This is what Paz is afraid of losing.

"What the hell?" I say when he gives me my phone back.

He gives me a level look. "Williams has an amazing English department."

"But what about Paz? Didn't you tell her you were staying close?"

"Well yeah, but—"

"So you are a shitty shoebox." But I smile as I say it.

Langston laughs and shakes his head, looking down at his feet. "I can't do what other people want all the time. My parents want me to be an engineer or a lawyer or whatever. Paz doesn't care, she just wants me close by, but what about what I want? I want to go to Williams. That's what I want. I shouldn't have told her I'd go to UBC."

"You need to make things right with her."

He nods. "Come on, we're going to be late."

. . .

Rumi picks me and Lyra up after tutoring. "Your one eye has a little splotch of brown," he says, peering close to my face. "I never noticed."

"It's called sectoral heterochromia. I didn't know for the longest time but the school nurse told me it's, like, an actual thing with a name."

Rumi has to do chores but he promises to let Lyra play his Switch when she's done with her tutoring homework. I get a delicious shiver thinking about the alone time we're going to get. No Lyra, nobody, just us.

I make myself some tea while we wait and Lyra is sitting at the table in a too-big T-shirt that says SAVE THE PANDAS and mismatching socks sagging around her skinny ankles with her homework spread out in front of her. I sit down with my mug in a patch of sunlight, hot through the smudged window.

"I saw my friend again. We had ice cream like he said maybe we could." She is a bit smug, like she thinks going out all by herself to have ice cream with a friend is a very grown-up thing to do. I also have a feeling this friend is a crush, so I nod and smile encouragingly without saying anything.

Lyra goes on, "And he was telling me about how he was watching this show that says nothing really matters, like there isn't any actual bad or good things."

"Huh," I say.

"And also maybe people don't really know."

"Know what?"

"Like what's really bad or good. Like there are things that are definitely bad like killing puppies or something but there's lots of things that are confusing and maybe people shouldn't be so annoying and bossy about right and wrong."

"But your aunt doesn't seem so bossy," I say.

"She never tells me what to do. I don't even have a bedtime. I stayed up until almost three again last night."

I never had a bedtime either. "So who's bossy then?"

"Rumi!" she shouts. "He is always telling me to do stuff."

"Is that bad?"

Lyra gives me a defiant look and shrugs. "I'm going to go find Trunks," she says, and abandons her homework. I feel like I should say something but I don't. I stare out the window and drink my tea and let my mind go blank. It's so nice to just sit and stare. I can't do this at home. There's always some noise, some chaos, some anxiety.

The screen door bangs open. "Rumi!" It's Lyra, screaming. She appears in the kitchen, frantic. Her eyes are wide and she has a skinned knee and mud on her shirt.

I stand up. "What's wrong?"

"Trunks is gone! He ran away!" Tears are streaming down her face. Even when she fell and scraped her knees and hands, she didn't cry. "Where's Rumi? I need to find him!"

But I don't know where he is. "I'll help you. Let's go." I follow her into the sun, running, dodging vines and pots and kneeling gardeners.

"He got out the back gate," she gasps. We run through the alley, and cars rush by the mouth, slicing through old puddles. "Trunks!" she's screaming, again and again.

"Trunks!" I yell, but there's no sign of him. We get to the intersection. Across the street is the trailhead. I watch the cars in between us and there. So many cars.

Lyra bends over at the waist, hands on her knees, breathing hard. She looks up at me, desperate, snot under her nose, tears making streaks on her dirty face.

I see a break in the cars. "Okay, let's go!" And we run for the trail. I text Rumi as we run.

on it, he texts back, *firefly is looking too!* I tell Lyra but she doesn't respond, she just keeps screaming his name. *Have you seen him? Have you seen him?* she asks every runner, biker, walker. Most of the time they ignore her but sometimes they shake their head. We have to be a mile away by now, but there's still no sign of him.

"Lyra," I start to say. "Lyra . . ."

She ignores me. Keeps running. Still crying. Gasping for breath.

"Lyra, maybe we should . . ." I say, but she doesn't stop.

"Lyra!" I grab her arm. "We've gone too far! He couldn't have made it this far."

"He could!" She whips around. "He's so fast! He loves this trail!"

"Maybe we should call the Humane Society," I say.

But she yanks away from me and starts running again.

"Lyra, stop! We have to stop!" I grab her again but she fights me, scrabbling to get away, so I wrap both my arms around her and hold tight. "We have to stop," I say again, and suddenly the yanking, straining, pulling stops and she sags into me.

"I need him," she weeps, face pressed into my shoulder. "I need him."

I guide her to a bench.

"He's lost," she cries. "He's alone and I don't want him to be scared, I don't want him to think I don't love him, I don't want him to think he doesn't have me anymore, he needs me, I need him, I'm scared without him, he keeps me safe, I keep him safe, he's my friend."

I wrap my arms around her and pull her to me, my hand on the back of her neck. Her hair is tangled and damp with sweat. "I know, I know, we'll find him, we'll find him," I say again and again and I'm thinking of the little match girl, the little half orphan, the boxcar child who doesn't even have a bedtime. Her only friend is a dog, a puppy who needs her as much as she needs him.

We walk back, arduously. Lyra weeps and calls his name and sits down a lot. Rumi's on the phone with the Humane Society and then Animal Control. He texts me as he goes. I promise to help Lyra make signs and tape them up everywhere, all over the city even, not just Wallingford. "People love dogs and he's such a sweet little puppy," I say. "Somebody will find him."

But she doesn't respond. We get to the trailhead and again I watch the cars rushing by, feeling all the anxiety of a tiny little puppy who might not be careful crossing the street. But there's nothing to indicate he might have been hit by a car. Then Lyra yelps and dashes out into the road and a car slams on its brakes, screeching to a stop, horn blaring. "Lyra!" I scream, and chase after her. A window comes down and somebody is yelling at me to watch my kid and I'm across the street at the mouth of the alley. She's crouching by a puddle and a pile of garbage and her arms are around something small and brown and furry and for a second I think Trunks is dead, he's been hit by a car, but then his head pops up out of her arms and he's licking her all over her face, licking her tears, and it's okay. He's okay.

Lyra dances through the alley. She switches from anguish to delight while I'm still holding my arms around myself to stop shivering. I texted Rumi that we found Trunks but he hasn't texted back in a while. I wonder if he's still out looking.

"Make sure you shut the gate this time," I say to Lyra.

And then Rumi comes out of the house.

"We found him!" Lyra calls, joyful. But he doesn't respond. His face is strange. He walks past me down the stairs and stands in the grass. He turns toward the orchard. The wind blows through the trees, the leaves, a sudden gust, and I watch the shadows play on his face.

"Poppy called," he says without looking at me.

"What?" I'm still in the echoes of losing Trunks.

"Poppy called," he says again.

"She called you?" I pull my phone out of my pocket but there's nothing. Why didn't she call me? "What did she say?"

He says, "She said she was sorry for disappearing."

I say, "What does that mean?"

And he says, "I don't know."

"Are you guys, I mean, are you still . . ." But I can't even say it. (Together.)

It's like I'm looking at him through a kaleidoscope. His smooth skin that is so warm. His eyes like tide pools, turning swirling greens and blues and grays. His curling dark hair tucked behind his ear. His broad straight nose and full upper lip.

He turns away. "I don't know," he says again, his back to me.

"What do you mean? What don't you know?"

"I don't know!" he says louder this time. "I feel guilty."

I take a step back.

In all those moments I never felt guilty.

I felt the space between us fill with promises.

Love, even.

"Guilty?" I say. "Guilty about what?"

"Everything," he says. "I told her about us."

"What did you say?"

My phone buzzes and I look down. It's Poppy calling.

"Hi," I say, breathless.

"Rumi says you've been hanging out. Like, a lot."

Her voice.

It's the same. It's exactly the way I remember it. It's visceral, this memory. Of hot skin, aerosol sunscreen, summer air that smells humid, together, together, the two of us, all of us, Poppy braiding her thick black hair over her copper-glow shoulder, over her teal bikini strap, legs in the water, summer after summer, together, together.

But she's gone. She left. She left me.

Her accusation hangs in the static space between us, waiting.

"Poppy, I can't believe you just left like that," I say.

"I was going to call."

"But you didn't."

"Virginia," she says, and she sounds exasperated. "I just, I couldn't . . . I needed . . ." she stammers, and I realize maybe she's stressed, not exasperated. Or maybe she's both. I can't tell. I can't tell what it is, what she's feeling. She's too far away from me.

She keeps going. "I needed some space. I can't explain it."

It's hard to answer that. I watch a fat bumblebee drift by. It passes near Rumi, who's standing there and pretending not to listen to me talk.

Rumi.

It hurts.

Rumi.

This moment hurts.

Caught in this space between Rumi and Poppy. And loving them both so much. Wanting them both so much.

She pauses. Then she says, "So, are you really hanging out with Rumi?"

"I mean, no." I laugh. I try to make it funny, but it doesn't work. "I ran into him at The Pearl a couple times and, you know, I tutor his sister but like . . . nothing's happening."

I feel Rumi's eyes on me as I lie to her. I remember the feel of his skin. I remember how close we came. I remember how we barely didn't. I remember how much I wanted to. I look at Rumi and I want to, right now, to kiss him, love him, declare myself for him. But I'm so afraid of losing her.

Why did she have to leave?

"Virginia," Poppy says. She sounds tired. Like she's rubbing her face. "I know you're lying to me."

I feel adrenaline in my hip flexors, the tops of my thighs. That strange rushing tightness deep in my muscles. "I can't believe this is what you called to talk to me about after all this time."

"I was going to call anyway," she says.

"If you hadn't left, none of this would have happened," I say.

"None of what would have happened?"

But I can't answer that.

"Why can't you just tell me the truth?" she says. "All I want you to do is talk to me. Just say the words."

My whole body aches to run, to race. "Say what words, though? I don't even know what you want me to say."

Her silence stretches and stretches and echoes and echoes and then she says, "Fuck you, Virginia." And then it's the dead flat sound of nothing because she hangs up the phone.

I don't think. I don't even know. I don't think I actually know what just happened. I don't think I can grasp it. Rumi is staring at me from far away. I feel like my vision is echoing. Vibrating. It's like looking through a flipbook. Like I'm looking at my life through a flipbook.

. . .

She already kind of left me, back at the beginning of the summer, when she went to her grandpa's. I don't know what I would do if she left me all the way. If she stopped being my friend.

I sit down on the grass. It's not unintentional like I'm feeling faint and I fall down. I don't lose control of my legs, my body. I wish I could lose control. I don't want to be in control. But I sit down because I guess I just don't care.

Rumi stands next to me, his legs next to my eyes, and I lose track of Lyra. I want him to sit next to me so much and then he does. "This is such a mess," Rumi says. He rubs his face and rests like that with his hands covering his eyes.

"Poppy left. She left me here," I say. "She left me here with nowhere to go, nowhere to escape to, nowhere to be safe." My voice is shaking. I want him to look at me, to see me, to take his hands from his eyes and wrap his arms around me and tell me I'm safe here with him. But he doesn't.

He just says, "I feel like a horrible person."

I wait and wait.

I hate waiting.

I hate myself for waiting.

I hate myself for not doing anything. I could end the waiting.

But what if I call and ask and the answer he gives me is bad?

What if I ask the question and he says no?

What if he says no?

What if he chooses Poppy?

Shouldn't he?

What if *she* chooses him, not me?

Not me, not me, not me.

Shouldn't she?

I'm just the bitch the slut the bad friend who interferes who injects herself into places into situations she doesn't belong. I'm just this bitch this whore this slut this bad friend.

So how can I do anything other than wait for my fate?

*O*nce upon a time there was this beautiful princess.
And she loved a prince. The princess, her name was
Sita. And the prince, his name was Rama. She lived in a
splendid and lavish palace that was cool in the summer
and dry throughout the many months of monsoons. Her
life was good, and everybody thought so.

Sita was so loyal and so devout that when her husband-
prince Rama was banished to the forests of Dandaka,
of course of course of course she followed him. And
when Rama told her to stay in their hut while he went on
adventures and he made a circle of salt around Sita and
told her to stay within it because within it she would be
safe, of course of course of course she listened.

When a poor wandering Brahmin dressed in ochre robes
came begging he lured her from her circle of salt. But it
was Ravana, a demon so terrible, he made the universe
scream. And then Sita was gone. Ravana spirited her
away to his fortress on the island of Sri Lanka. For a year
he raged. Like a willow bending in the wind she resisted.

Ravana had many faces. Sometimes he wore his face
with gentle eyes. Sometimes he wore his terrible face, his
lunatic face, his violent face, his hateful face. Sometimes
he wore his saddest face: How could Sita be so cruel?
He only loved her and wanted her. But the worst was his

gentle face. It was hard to resist the soft and kind eyes even though she knew what other faces Ravana wore.

She couldn't sleep. She was too scared. Sometimes she hid but he always found her. Sometimes she lied but he always knew. After a while she felt powerless, so she waited. Her only power was to resist his many faces. Her only power was to wait. Because she knew that her prince, her Rama, would come. She knew Rama would move mountains and part the waters of the ocean to free her from Ravana. And Rama did come for her. He fought Ravana's armies and he killed Ravana and freed Sita and brought her home to their splendid and lavish palace.

And because of Sita's devotion, because of her loyalty, because of how she waited, they lived happily ever after. Right?

Thirteen

MY PHONE IS ringing. It wakes me up. It's not even seven in the morning. It's Rumi. I haven't talked to anybody for hours and hours. Not since yesterday when Poppy called Rumi and I left because he kept not looking at me. And all the rest of the day the whole time I kept thinking Poppy would call or at least text but she didn't.

"Hey," I say. I lie back on the pillow and close my eyes with the phone resting on my cheek.

"Hey, I need a favor." He sounds upset, stressed. "I fucked up."

"What? What happened?" I rub my eyes.

"I'm such an asshole. I forgot I have to take Lyra to this soccer thing today and I took a shift at work and now I can't get out of it and my aunt can't do it because she has her board meeting and it's like an all-day thing, you have to take the ferry out to Bremerton and everything." He's talking fast and I can hear him thumping around, pacing maybe. "I'm so mad at myself. I can't believe I forgot. She even reminded me a couple days ago and I just wasn't paying attention."

"It's okay, it's okay. I don't have anything going on today, I don't think." Do I? No. I don't. "Yeah, I can do it."

"Oh god thank you so much. I feel like such an asshole forgetting this. It's so important to her. I'll come get you. Can I pick you up in thirty minutes? You have to be at the ferry to meet up with the other parents at nine."

"Shit. Fuck. Yes. I'm getting up. I'm getting dressed right now," I say.

He pauses. "Wait, you can drive, right?"

"Yes!"

"Okay, you can take my car for the day. I can take the bus to work. It will be fine."

"It will be fine. I'll see you soon," I say.

But when he picks me up it isn't fine. He looks at me in a particular way. Like he's sad. Lyra is in the back seat with her big headphones on. The music is so loud, I can hear the little tinny words all the way over here. I think she's listening to the Spice Girls. I tilt my head and listen and then sing, "If you wanna be my lova, you gotta get with my friends!" and waggle my eyebrows at him, but he doesn't laugh. He just looks away.

Outside there is a blue jay on a tree. It squawks once, then again. I take a sip of my coffee and keep my face turned away. It's hot through the cardboard cup. It's burning my hand.

"You have insurance, right?" Rumi says.

"Yes. And my driver's license," I say, smiling small.

He nods at the steering wheel.

"It's going to be fine. Lyra will be fine. I won't crash your car. We'll be okay."

He nods some more, then looks at me. "I know. Thank you," he says.

As soon as we get to the upper deck of the ferry Lyra bounces up to a group of adolescents with ribbons in their hair and numbers painted on their cheeks. I sink down into my bench and bend over my phone.

"Hiya," He says. He's smiling at me. Standing there. "Are you with Lyra today?"

It's Him. Him. He's coaching?

"Her aunt couldn't come and then Rumi, her brother, got called in to work and couldn't miss it." I keep my face blank. I don't show anything. There's nothing here. I'm empty.

"Oh yeah? Are you and Rumi friends?" He's still smiling at me.

I shrug. I disavow Rumi. "I mean, I tutor Lyra and they needed help, so."

"Right on," He says. He puts His hand on my shoulder and squeezes.

I just want Him to go. Just go. I rub my middle finger with my thumb.

He turns and leaves and then rushes to the group of girls making a noise like a low rumbling growl, arms out, bent low, and then roars loud, louder and louder, and the girls scream and jump and run away and He herds them to a big circle of chairs to do team building or something, I guess. I examine Lyra's face. She's laughing, looking delighted.

I straighten my neck. Look forward. At nothing. I rub my finger. And then out the window. Down at the water. I count the jellyfish bobbing in the dark gray, the foaming white waves, the arrows in the wake.

We all drive in a big caravan to a pristine soccer field up a bluff from the Puget Sound. I drive with the windows down, and the air coming in smells like sweet blackberries and wet earth. Lyra leans her head out the window, her hair flying like a tangled windsock behind her. But I wander the edge of the field while they do their thing. The girls. The parents. Him. I skid down to the rocky little beach and smell the salt and seaweed and close my eyes so the sun is red and glowing through my eyelids.

On the way back I make Lyra sit with me. Stress feels sour in my stomach like I might puke it up. So I get a tea and no food and I buy Lyra a hot chocolate with whipped cream and sprinkles and a cream cheese and cherry Danish and try my best to distract her. To keep her occupied. Keep her away from Him.

She likes it when I ask her questions. "Which would you choose, sneezing every time you asked a question no matter what forever," I say, and Lyra leans in, grinning in anticipation. "Or never being able to tell the difference between a baby and a muffin?"

She screeches and claps her hands over her mouth, looking

side to side like one of those old Felix clocks. "Definitely snee-
zes! I like sneezing. Sometimes I make myself sneeze."

"How?"

"I stick a piece of grass up my nose."

I make a face and she laughs and I notice that Lyra is twirling
a ring around her middle finger.

"What is that?" I say. "A mood ring?"

Lyra blushes and nods and I rub my thumb against a phan-
tom chafe at the base of my middle finger.

Lyra looks over my shoulder. The light from the windows high-
lights the tiny hairs on her cheek, and dust motes swirl in the air
in front of her and she smiles and lifts up her hand.

I look behind me. It's Him. He smiles. He walks over. I watch
His feet. Black running shoes. Some high-end brand.

He puts His hand on Lyra's shoulder.

She quirks her small body. Turns herself toward Him. Aligns
her spine with His.

Her mood ring glitters and I touch the base of my finger.

I touch the ghost of a ring.

They talk about going to get ice cream. Together. Alone. Just
the two of them. Their special time.

Her friend. Her friend. Her special friend. Her soccer coach.
It's Him. It's Him.

He smiles and touches her cheek. She smiles as He touches
her cheek.

I touch my finger. I rub it. It hurts, where there used to be a ring, but it's not there anymore.

He talks to me.

He is still touching Lyra. His hand lingers on her neck.

I talk back. I say words. He says words.

He leaves.

Lyra is blushing. Smiling. Looking down at her mood ring.

The trees and the sun and the bright houses and the wind light on my skin. I let it all come into sharp focus and pay attention to those things instead of what I know now. There's nobody on the narrow cracked road, on the wide sidewalk grouted with grass and dandelions. I drive past coffee shops and smoke shops and cell phone stores and teriyaki joints and I park in front of the old farm house funny and beautiful in this big gray city.

I get out. I walk around the car. I gather Lyra's soccer things. She bounces behind me, chattering. I look at her. Her bird bones. Her skinny wrists and shoulder blades pointing through her soccer jersey. I feel like I am gasping for breath. But I'm not. I'm like a double-exposed photograph. Blank face. Empty. Nothing. Also screaming and gasping and clutching myself.

Her eyes are big and brown. They're not like Rumi's. Rumi's are green and strange and the color of the ocean on a bright sunny day. Lyra's eyes are the color of a coffee bean and they gleam bright always. She turns to go and I want to hug her, hold her tight to me, protect her small body, but I can't, I can't touch her. I can't put my hands on her.

I can't believe I have to do this.

Rumi jogs down the stairs. He smiles at me. Even after Poppy. Even. Even. Even.

Oh god. I don't know if I can do this. I'm shaking. I can't keep my hands still. They're shaking.

"How did it go?" he says.

"Rumi," I say. My lips are numb. My fingertips are tingling. It's been so long since I've said His name. I don't want to. I hate saying His name.

"What? What's wrong? Virginia?"

I sink to my knees and put my head in my hands. The grass is damp. My knees sink into the old rain, the mud. Rumi's voice is behind my head, just past my thoughts, my awareness. His hands are hot on my back. "Virginia," he's saying, "Virginia." He pulls me up to standing. I let him guide me to the stairs.

I look at him. At Rumi. He has been so good at this. At me. I can. I can tell him. Lyra is standing in the yard watching us, Trunks rolling in the mud at her feet. Her ponytail is lopsided, loose, hanging just over her left ear.

"I have to tell you something," I say.

"Okay," he says.

"The thing is, there's this person and He like . . . I mean, He actually." I stop and suck in a breath. "Remember when I said I don't like to sleep in my house? Because bad things happen in the dark? Well, it's because. I don't know if you guessed. That.

I was." I'm being incoherent and Rumi is staring at me like I'm crazy. Lyra is down there. I can feel her watching. She's being so quiet because she's probably trying really hard to hear what I'm saying. I lower my voice.

"So there's actually one person who does that. It's not people. It's one person. He, I'm worried that He . . . I'm worried about Lyra." I don't even think Rumi's grasping what I'm saying, because he just looks confused.

"You're worried about me?" Lyra says, loud on the stairs. "Why are you worried about me?"

"You don't need to worry about Lyra," Rumi says.

I turn and look at her. At her small self. "No, listen. Seriously, Rumi, Lyra isn't safe right now."

"What do you mean I'm not safe? What are you talking about?" She's even louder now.

"I don't know what you're talking about," Rumi says. He stands up and I stand up too. I'm on a step lower than him, so I'm looking up at him as he says, "Lyra is fine. She *is* safe." That emphasis on *is*. She *is* safe. She *is*. He turns to go up the stairs, inside the house, away from me.

"Rumi, seriously. Just fucking stop for a second!" I follow him.

He whips his head around and I realize that I swore in front of Lyra. She's still lingering at the bottom of the stairs and now me and Rumi are on the porch. "I'm really worried about Lyra!" I say.

"Well, stop! She's fine! I'm taking care of her and I'm not going to let anything happen to her, so just don't worry about it," Rumi says.

"What are you talking about?" Lyra says. "Rumi, what is she talking about?"

"Mind your business," he snaps at her.

"This obviously *is* my business!" she yells.

"But you *are* letting something happen to her! You're not paying attention to her! You don't even notice that she sneaks out all the time! She's bored and lonely and desperate for attention! He's grooming her!"

Rumi's face changes. His skin turns red and it's like his every muscle is strained. "You need to go."

It's like a wave of white noise crashes into my brain. Like shock and numbness and fuzz. He's not listening to me. "You're not listening to me."

"Seriously, you need to leave."

I feel her move behind me and I look at her. At her messy hair that needs a comb, at her dingy white soccer shirt, at her untied shoes, at her skinny legs and grass-stained knees. And then I look back at Rumi. "You're just going to let it happen."

I don't think I've ever seen actual rage in his face, but it's there now. "I would never let anything happen to her!" he yells, and I stumble back. "Lyra is safe, I'm right here, she is fine and you need to leave!"

And so I do. And I shake all the way home.

My empty house is dark and cold and smells stale.

In a box. Under my bed. Surrounded by dust bunnies and Barbie dolls and empty bottles of nail polish.

In a box, in a sparkly pink piece of tissue paper gift wrapped just for me.

A mood ring set in sterling silver, a dull glimmer in the gloom. It's black because it's cold.

It's just heat that makes it turn colors. It's not my mood. It's not my feelings.

It's in the palm of my hand and I think about it and then I try. I try to put it on my middle finger where I used to wear it, but now it won't fit. It won't fit because I'm bigger now. It's made for an adolescent. For an eleven-year-old. I was eleven when He gave it to me.

Lyra is eleven. He gave her a mood ring. He kept touching her. He kept touching her. He didn't stop.

He didn't stop after me. He didn't stop.

I don't cry, I just rock. I just wrap my arms around my legs and press my face into my knees and rock in my dark room alone clutching this mood ring.

Fourteen

THERE IS A crow in the street picking at a smashed-flat squirrel. It tugs hard at skinny entrails until they break, snapping like a rubber band. There is a lot of smoke in my lungs and I blow it out aiming for the crow. I turn my phone over in my hands.

are you coming? Ro texts. I flick the butt of my joint into the gutter.

I need to talk to you, Ro texts.

Virginia seriously, come meet me at the party, please?

My head hurts with it, the not wanting. How much I don't want to move. How much I don't want to do anything at all at all at all. My eyes are hot. My face is sweating.

is rumi there? I text her back.

haven't seen him

But that doesn't mean he won't be there. I don't know if I want to see him or not.

So when I get there I find a beer and then I look for Ro. The danger is that I will trip while walking because I'm not looking where I'm going. I'm just looking for Rumi. I slurp deep into my beer. Flat warm foam on my lip. Not enough though, I need more. Edison and Thalia are nuzzling each other in the kitchen. Paz and Langston are playing Mario and taking bong hits. Poppy isn't here of course. I finish the beer quick and keep looking for Ro.

where are you? I text.

She's in the backyard on a swing. I sit on the swing next to her. Every part of me feels heavy. I should tell Ro about Lyra. But Ro has tears shimmering in her eyelashes. "Hannah won't tell them," she says.

It takes me a second to catch up. I spin my swing around so our knees are touching. "She won't tell her parents?"

"Virginia." She stops and scrunches her eyes shut. A few tears leak out. She wipes her cheeks and looks at me. "I told her I loved her."

"Oh, Ramona." I pull her into an awkward tangled hug and she presses her face to my neck and I feel her shuddering with sobs.

"I told her that I loved her and it didn't matter to her. She still won't tell her parents."

"God," I say.

"I've never told anyone that before," Ro says. Her tears drip onto my legs.

Nobody is looking at us. Drinking their beers in their red Solo cups looking the other way. But then, it's not that unusual to cry in the dark at a party. Ro's heart breaks into mine and I can't tell her about Lyra. I just can't summon the breath.

And then, just like Ro, she strips off her pain and shakes out her braids. I hold my phone to her face so she can check her makeup. "Okay, I'm done," she says. "Let's go howl at the moon."

And so we troll around the party dredging up shit to talk and beers to drink. She's just pretending, but so am I.

"Seriously, did you hear, though?" Ro says.

I drink more and look at Ro over the rim of my cup. "Hear what?" I say.

"About Poppy and Rumi. Did she tell you?"

"Did they break up?" I say. She thinks, of course, Poppy would tell me a big thing like that. Because Ro doesn't know about Poppy and me and our fight.

But then Ro yanks my arm and points at Liz because she has tripped in on high high heels. Liz has the uncomfortable look of a girl whose outfit works when she's posing in front of a mirror but not when she starts moving. Her shirt needs to be tugged down, her skirt keeps riding up, and her hair needs to be combed.

"She looks like a baby deer." I mime learning to walk.

Ro laughs and I feel mean, but I don't care.

Then Ro says, "Virginia," but I stop listening because Liz has tottered over to Rumi (where did he come from?) and her hand is possessively on his arm and he doesn't look properly affronted and I can't understand why not, because he and I, at least I thought, even though we had that fight, even though I said he didn't pay enough attention to Lyra, and if he and Poppy broke up, I mean, I know we're not together yet, but I thought, I thought.

He doesn't look at me as she kisses him, but his cheeks turn ruddy and he tugs her away, out of sight, and she is smiling like she has no fucking idea.

And then I become aware of Ro and quite a few others staring at me, waiting, wanting to know.

What I thought it was is not what it was. I can feel the realization on my face, on display for everybody to see.

I feel a surge of anger. Because I am devastated and embarrassed and confused and being stared at, and that is the worst possible combination of things to be. Rumi is no longer in the room, so who am I trying to save face for?

Ro and Paz follow me across the room and out the door. They sit on either side of me on the front steps.

"What the fuck?" Ro says.

"Right?" Paz agrees. "What happened to him and Poppy?" She looks at me. "Do you know what happened?"

Ro is watching me too. She says, "Okay, what I was trying to tell you before? Was that I heard he and Poppy maybe broke up? She found out you guys were hanging out a lot? And you guys had a fight? Like, you and Poppy?" She keeps ending her sentences in question marks, but I'm not answering.

"Did you guys fight?" Paz says to me.

"Me and Poppy?" I say.

"Yeah," Paz says.

"Yeah, I guess we did."

"But she's the one who disappeared," Ro says, and I press my shoulder into hers.

"And they broke up?" I say.

Ro nods. "That's what I heard," she says.

"We thought if Rumi and Poppy broke up, and I mean, of

course they would, she left him too. She left everybody," Paz says. "But anyway, we thought if they broke up, you two would end up together. You and Rumi. He seemed so, like, in love with you."

(*Seemed,* she said. Past tense.)

"Right, but now he's dating Liz?" Ro says. "Like, what the fuck? Isn't she a sophomore?"

I nod. She was in my tour group when she came to Elderberry as a freshman.

"What is he even doing?" Ro says.

I can't stand it suddenly and cover my face with my hands. It's because of what I said about Lyra. I know it is.

I need to be alone. I am going to cry. I can't cry. I can't cry in front of all these people. I can't smear my makeup and look like Rocky Raccoon and look like a psycho and look like I actually finally cared about some guy and then he went and totally fucking fucked me over. I need to be alone.

I need to be alone, I think I say or maybe I just think it as I stumble to the bathroom and stare into the mirror at my stupid face and my stupid body and my stupid heart and my stupid self. I stare and stare and stare and I feel like I am moving farther and farther away from myself until I don't even recognize the person standing in the mirror and she's just some normal-looking broad with dyed hair and lots of eyeliner and bony shoulders and guys probably only like her because she has big boobs and shows them around with her skinny tank tops and lacy bralettes.

She backs away from the mirror and straightens her shirt and checks out her butt and smiles at herself on the way out the door.

I am hyperaware of my limbs. My arms swinging, my shorts swishing over my legs, my fingers twitching. My skin feels too tight for my body.

I find Rumi in the den.

"Where's Liz?" I say.

He shrugs and looks at me like, *Really, we're doing this?*

Like I am standing outside of myself, it is hard to understand the pain that shivers across my rib cage. Can't Rumi understand it? He has been so good at understanding my feelings.

I think these things show on my face, because he shifts his eyes just a little but enough. He is denying my reaction, denying that I had expectations, denying the implications of all those sunlit days, smoky nights, the mingling of limbs, the secrets we told.

The falling, just short of love.

He sighs and rubs his neck still not looking at me. And it occurs to me that he doesn't want to be here, looking away from me but still standing across from me. He doesn't want to deal with the pain and confusion that must be radiating from me like an odor. He wants to leave. And then I scramble. Wait. *Can't* we be friends?

Can't I still hope? Maybe after. Maybe later. Maybe maybe maybe.

Or maybe not.

"You're such an asshole," I say.

He looks down. He doesn't say anything. He (and now the pain is sharp) walks away without ever looking at me again. Without ever talking to me. Trying really hard to act like it's no big deal. He's just meandering over there to talk to so-and-so and Virginia is fine just fine.

I turn and turn and turn again and find nowhere to land.

"Virginia!" Ro waves me over and I go to her like a drowning person to a lifeboat.

The night trails away into stinging shots and withheld tears. I don't remember coming home, but now I lie in bed and stare at Anansi and the room tilts and stutters and now that I am alone and I want them to come, the tears won't come and I feel such very deep sadness, so I take a handful of melatonin and drink some wine and will myself into denial and sleep.

*O*nce upon a time.

No I can't I just can't.

Fifteen

I CAN'T BELIEVE *you told rumi i sneak out all the time,* Lyra texts. *hes super mad.*

good, I text back. *you shouldn't be sneaking out*

he can't stop me anyway, she says.

Lyra seriously don't meet up with that guy, with your friend

But she doesn't respond.

I have a leftover half a joint from last time Rumi and I . . . The last time we were in his room. In his bed. I remember how my arm was behind his neck. I remember how he curled into me, like he wanted me to hold him. I remember the smoke curling out of my mouth, how it looked beautiful in the lamp light. I remember how I passed him the joint and he told me to keep it. How his face, for a minute, was impish and how his dimple showed even though he wasn't smiling. I put the joint on his table and then I put it in a little baggie the next day and I didn't smoke it. How I saved it like a keepsake.

I find it now and light it and smoke it all down. Down until it burns my fingers and I flick it out into the rain.

Ro texts. She asks me how I am. I don't respond to that and

ask her about Hannah instead. She says she hasn't talked to her. They're on a de facto break while Ro sorts out her feelings. She is agonizing: *quelle horreur,* she texts. I send her a bunch of hearts. She says we'll meet up later.

Paz texts. She tells me she's coming over with burritos and bubbly water.

you know the way to a girls heart, I reply.

I hold my phone over my face, examining myself in the camera. I am haggard. I get up and wash my face and knot my hair up to hide the grease. I brush my teeth. I glance at the tarnished mirror above the sink. I look slightly less dead than I did before.

For a minute I stare at my reflection.

I can't believe this is where I am. I can't believe this is what I'm feeling.

Paz finds me back in bed. Washing my face drained me.

"So what's going on with Langston," I say through a mouthful of burrito.

Paz shakes her head.

"It's fine!" I say. "I can handle it. Just talk."

"Well obviously, if he gets into Williams he's going to go. If he applies early decision he's obligated to."

I nod and hand her the bubbly water. "There might be some burrito backwash in there."

She holds it up to the light. "Nope, all good. Anyway, so we've been talking, like a lot, I mean you know me."

"Right."

"And I think, well, I think it's going to be fine. He really wants to stay together even though we'll be super far apart. I was so worried that he would want to, you know, fuck around."

I wrap my arm around her waist and pull her into me. "He loves you so much," I say. "Your relationship is what I wish I had. He adores you."

Paz rubs her eyes. "He's the only one I've ever been with. I'm so afraid of losing him, Virginia."

"You're not going to lose him. And even if you did, even if you do lose him, even if you guys break up, you're smart and sweet and incredibly kind and honestly the most beautiful girl I've ever actually known in real life. If you guys do break up? Paz, you won't be diminished. You will be okay. I have total faith in you to be okay no matter what. But I don't think you'll break up. I think Langston knows how beautiful and amazing you are and doesn't want to lose you. I think he just wants to go to Williams."

"Well, it's not like we're going to be together forever. I know that. I just don't want to break up anytime soon." She laughs a little. "Anyway. How are you?"

"I don't know," I say. "I don't care."

"Virginia," Paz says.

"What?"

"You definitely care."

I bite my lip. "Have you seen them?"

"Yeah, I saw them." Paz pushes her feet against my leg and lies back on my pillow with her head next to mine.

"Where?" I finally manage.

"They were at The Pearl."

"Together? Or just because he was working?"

"I think she was waiting for him."

I wait for Paz to go on but she doesn't.

"And then what?"

She sighs and pushes her forehead into my neck. "Virginia," she says again.

"What?"

"I don't think Liz is the problem."

I find Anansi. He's migrated to the corner above my bookshelf.

"You're right," I say, and change the subject.

I keep texting Lyra. But she doesn't respond. Or she responds with pictures or emojis or GIFs. A dancing hairless cat. Trunks chasing a ball. A pumpkin emoji and a Christmas tree and a moon. I stare at them all together, studying them, trying to find the code, the magic spell, the hidden pattern.

But now we have tutoring. Lyra is blithe, resistant, pretending nothing has changed. Then she asks, "So when can you come over again?" as I walk out with her.

Rumi is waiting in his car. He's just sitting and staring at his phone. He doesn't look up. He doesn't look up, stubbornly, like he's refusing to look up.

But Lyra doesn't go over there. She just stands here still talking to me. She says, "Because I think Trunks is almost trained.

I mean, he peed in the house again yesterday but he also sits when I tell him to!"

I turn from Rumi to her. "That's great."

"So can you come over?" she says. She just wants things to go back to normal.

Rumi slams the door and starts walking over, head down, hands in his pockets.

"I don't know," I tell Lyra. I can't keep my eyes off Rumi. "I'm not sure I can."

"Like, at all?" Lyra says, and I look back at her. "Like you can't come, at all? Ever?"

"Is that man, your soccer coach, is He your friend? The one that you hang out with sometimes?"

Lyra looks away from me. She says, "I don't know what you're talking about."

"Lyra, seriously, don't spend time with Him."

"When can we hang out? When can you come back over?" she says.

But I just shake my head and shrug at her as I feel Rumi watching me.

"Why?" she demands. "Why can't you?"

"Lyra," Rumi says. "Where's your backpack?"

She gives me a look of such hurt it echoes and vibrates in my head, and then she turns and walks back into the community center.

Rumi still won't look at me. He's wearing a nice shirt. It looks soft. It's light blue with red dots, tiny red dots, and it buttons up and the top two buttons are open and I can see his skin. And his hair is combed and silky. He's dressed up nice like he's going on a date with Liz. A real official date. A thing we never did. A thing I never even thought of as a possibility. Where are they going? Dinner and a movie?

Lyra comes slinking back, staring at her phone. Rumi heads to his car.

"Lyra," I say.

She looks back at me, sullen, already accepting that I'm going to abandon her too, just like everybody else. "What?" she says.

"I just . . ." I start, but then she looks down at her phone and I do too.

It's a text from Kermit the Frog. I quirk my head, trying to see better. "Is that," I say. It is. It is. It's Him. He made me save His number as a cartoon character too. He was Perry the Platypus in my phone. Like it was just friends being dumb. Like it was just a joke.

Lyra quickly puts her phone in her pocket and ignores me, hurrying to the car. I follow her. I breathe, I breathe, I breathe, and still I feel like I might pass out anyway. Like I can't get enough oxygen. Like my pharynx and larynx and trachea and lungs might not be working properly. "Lyra," I say, and she hurries faster. "Lyra wait, wait, don't, don't text Him, Lyra, wait." But she won't stop, she won't listen, she walks around the car and gets in the passenger seat.

Rumi is sitting there, window up, staring at his phone, they're about to drive away, the two of them, ignoring me. I knock. He won't look at me. I want to break his window. I knock again, harder, louder. "Open your window!" I shout, letting my temper surge.

Slowly and only a fraction, his window comes down.

"I need to talk to you."

"Virginia," he says, like this is painful for him.

My head feels full of static, buzzing. I press my fingers to my forehead and close my eyes and I take a step back.

I need his help to do this. Please just help me. Rumi. Please just help me.

But he drives away as though my step back was permission.

I feel like throwing my phone across the parking lot, watching it land, watching it shatter. But I don't.

*O*nce upon a time there was this woman. She was held captive by these horrible people, these pirates, these ogres, these monsters, these beasts.

And then something amazing and magical happened. She fell in love with a prince. The prince saved her. He rescued her from the beasts who held her captive and so she showed him her truest her deepest her most secret self. Because finally finally finally she was safe.

The prince pretended to love her back but he didn't really. He didn't love her. And so she fell victim once more to the beasts and that's it. That's the end of her story because happy endings don't exist. They're not real. They're fake. The end.

Sixteen

I WAKE UP vibrating. The room is slanted and dark. The motion stops and I focus on the blurry shape crawling across my ceiling until the image sharpens and I realize it is Anansi. He stops. The vibrating starts again.

My phone is under my pillow. *trunks hasnt peed in three days!!!* Lyra texts me.

i mean like in the house or anything, she says.

like hes peed just hes peed outside

we got him a little chewy cheeseburger that he chews on

also a rubber fish

She sends me a video of him fetching a ball and another one of him sitting. In it she screams, "Sit!" like a deranged drill sergeant and he wobbles his little butt down. I watch and I press my smile into the heel of my hand.

that's great, I text her back, and I stare at the glowing phone in my hand, wanting to ask about Him. Wanting to ask if she is texting Him, seeing Him. But I dread her answer. Or if she doesn't answer me, I dread that too.

I lie back and close my eyes because my heart is beating hard and fast and it's like I can't breathe. There's a bottle of half-drunk beer next to me. It's warm and flat and sour. I drink it all the way down.

Something bangs on my window and I startle, clutching the bottle to my chest. But it's just Ro, balancing on a branch of the maple. It squeals, scraping against the window, bending under her weight.

I wrench the window open. The screen is still on the floor from when I snuck out when He was here.

Ro clambers in, a bright forced smile on her face. "Bonjour! Comment ça va? Ils nous attendant! Allons-y!" Ro says, like I'm supposed to be wherever I'm not.

"What? What's wrong?" I say.

"There's a party," she says. "Remember?"

"Ro, what's wrong? Don't be fake."

Her body loses all its tension. She unspools onto my bed like a cut guitar string. I lie down next to her and cover us both with my purple quilt.

"Is it Hannah?" I say.

Ro pushes her face into my neck and her answer is muffled. "I think it's over, like for real."

"Ro," I croon, wrapping my arms around her. "Do you want to talk about it?"

"I can't tell if I'm being an asshole for making this a deal breaker, that she won't tell her parents about me, or if it's okay for me to draw this line. I know how she comes out is up to her. I do know that. But the idea of being with somebody who's keeping me a secret, it's just gross, you know?"

"I think that's valid. You aren't telling her she has to tell her parents. You're telling her you don't want to be in a relationship with somebody who isn't out. I feel like even though it's hard and it sucks, that's okay. *You* get to decide what your needs are. *You* get to decide what kind of relationship you want to be in."

"But maybe I should just give her more time."

"But does the idea of that make you feel gross?" I say.

"Yeah," Ro says, and closes her eyes.

"I think you have good instincts, Rowie. I think you should listen to them."

"I'm just really sad," Ro says. She lies like that, eyes closed, tears clinging to her lashes, her mouth an eloquent bow bending with sorrow. Her pain echoes between us, back and forth.

"I'm sorry you're sad," I say after a while.

"Okay, but they're waiting for us, so let's go."

"Don't you want to just not go? Let's watch *Scream*. Blood and guts make everything better."

"I'm not just going to wallow," Ro says, standing up.

"Ro," I start.

"Nope. You're not going to wallow either. Let's go."

Ro keeps talking and I start getting changed and my hand somehow picks the things that show the most of the skin I can't stand to be in, the tiniest top and the shortest shorts. Ro climbs out the window and it's like I am not in control of my body. I climb and jump and land and everything is fine just fine just fine.

It is hard to be here. I don't feel like a normal teenager getting drunk getting high having fun. I feel like I'm going crazy. I feel like there is a white noise screaming in my head while I'm standing here laughing at Paz and Ro's witty banter.

"I need alcohol," I say, "it's the only reason I came." And I laugh when Ro looks at me worried and Paz leads the way to the kitchen, and her eyes flick to where Thalia and Edison are standing, looking away from each other. Edison is holding a Solo cup waiting to fill it up at the keg. Thalia is looking like the kind of unhappy that takes up so much energy, there's none left to hide it. She has dark circles under her eyes. I realize I'm staring and turn back to Paz and Ro.

But my eyes keep wandering over to Thalia. Edison disappears and she smiles anemically at Rand's funny, funny jokes. She frowns at the beer in her hand and doesn't drink it at all until she shakes her head and downs it in several big gulps.

There is something about her tonight.

She reminds me of someone.

Me.

She reminds me of me.

Rand starts touching her stomach, poking and prodding, saying, "Where'd all your muscles go? You're getting a little rotund. You used to be so fit," and pinching and probing. Thalia isn't moving. She isn't protesting. She's just staring into some fuzzy middle distance with blank eyes. Rand keeps doing it, past the point at which I figure he would stop because he's being inappropriate and invasive and even a handsome charming white dude should have some sense of propriety.

But he doesn't. Rand keeps touching her stomach. It takes

Paz all of about fifteen seconds to yell "Stop touching her!" and yank his hand away. Langston appears next to her looking serious and proper and protective and Rand laughs with his hands held up in front of him.

"Sorry." He walks away still laughing. Paz shakes her head after him and Langston wraps an arm around her waist and Thalia looks at me still standing with Ro.

"Where's Edison?" Ro says.

I shrug.

I saw it happening before Paz did.

Why didn't I say something?

Why don't I ever say anything?

I'm bending over to pull a beer out of the fridge when some junior makes a wet fart noise and his dumb friends laugh. I grin and shake my ass and tilt the beer back. Swallow swallow swallow. Fart-boy high-fives me as I leave swinging my hips just right.

Ro and Paz have scattered and I feel like my safe haven has scattered with them. Langston is still standing with Thalia but they are both staring at their phones, not talking. Edison is across the room watching me. I make eye contact and flush, hating myself for caring.

I take a drink for something to do and choke on my beer, coughing and sputtering. Brett and Isaiah laugh and I faux-scowl. I clink my bottle against Brett's, saying "Cheers," like I'm toasting my own stupidity. Brett fingers the lacy bottom of my shirt, letting his hand brush against my skin. He makes some joke/excuse for touching me and I laugh along with everybody else. I laugh when Isaiah pokes me in the ribs, making me jump and squeal. I laugh when Rand tilts my beer while I'm taking a drink and I dribble a little down my chin. I laugh when Tobias dares two sophomore girls to make out and they do and I laugh when Edison jeers and I laugh when they stumble and break apart and wipe their mouths and look proud and embarrassed at the same time. I laugh when Rand grabs Marcela's breasts from behind and she elbows him in the stomach, blushing and laughing, and sticks her tongue out, making a sexy/goofy Instagram face. I laugh when Brett presses a cold beer to my bare back and tells me to drink up.

And so I do. I drink and laugh and drink and laugh and every time somebody degrades me I laugh and every time some other girl gets degraded I laugh. I drink until it's hard to focus and it's impossible to care.

Edison smiles at me as I pass him on the way to the bathroom, trailing his fingers along my ribs that peek out from under my hoochie crop. A trail of goose bumps burn in the wake of his touch. I give him a sideways glance and I give him a tiny corner of a sneaky smile.

I text Edison while I pee: *your a cunt*
He texts back right away: *you're**
fuck you
no darling fuck you
shall we?
lets

I decide I've had enough of this party and stumble out the front door. Technicolor spots dance in front of my eyes as I walk into the streetlights.

I hear Edison walking behind me.

My house is just around the corner.

My parents are gone.

I wait for him in the backyard.

There is no dance. Only the undressing. I stand in the hot summer night air but the heat doesn't penetrate. I am cold. My bones are cold.

My shorts puddle around my feet. I take off my shirt, his eyes all over my skin.

I can see his erection through his shorts.

His lips on my neck. A sour kiss. Like rotten fruit.

My head might be a balloon. A red helium balloon. It floats away toward the oak. Lodges in the leaves. They are dim and gray in the dark and rustle so I can't hear anything. The red string trails beneath the branches in tight spirals.

Then he touches me and I am back. I get goose bumps, but they are cold like an ice cube on my skin.

He puts his hand between my legs and I lie down, pulling him on top of me, wrapping my legs around him, pressing into his erection.

I know all the moves.

I shimmy his shorts off with my feet. We kiss. He tastes like menthol cigarettes and Diet Pepsi. He pushes his tongue deeper into my mouth and I master the urge to gag. He starts to move down but I don't want him to, so I arch my hips and he pulls off my underwear. I spit into my hand and get myself wet. He starts off slow but I roll him over and get on top and go fast. I really fuck him. I pretend to orgasm. I tell him I'm coming I'm coming I'm coming and gasp and moan and grab fistfuls of my own hair and really put on a show.

"I'm going to come, Virginia," he moans.

I hate the sound of my name in his mouth.

I finish him off with my hand. Normally I would give him a blow job, but I just can't. He tastes like Clorox and asparagus. I would puke. I wipe his semen on the grass. I return to the balloon. He starts texting and from far away I watch.

"Okay bye," I think he says. Maybe not. Maybe he just leaves. There is no dignity in this.

I lie in my cold backyard. The windows of my house light up. My parents must be home. I wonder if they realize I'm out here. Or if they wonder where I am. I wonder if they care.

I know it's a bad idea, but I pull my phone out and scroll up up up to where Rumi's messages are long and full of implications.

I feel the tears in my throat first. When they emerge, I'm ready for them, hands already covering my face, but the intensity of my grief is surprising. I'm shaking and my arms are wrapped around myself like maybe I can hold myself together, stop myself from shaking to pieces. I am not prepared for this.

I'm sobbing, my face pressed into my knees so nobody can hear my keening. I don't understand, I didn't even ever have Rumi, it was all just fake, I was just pretending. It's not even about him. I don't even know what it's about.

But I do actually.

It's not about Rumi it's about how alone I am it's about how I have nobody to tell it's about Him.

He didn't stop after me.

He didn't stop.

So that Medea story, it wasn't all of it. (But you already knew that, didn't you?) They didn't live happily ever after. (Nobody does.)

When Jason came and he asked for the Golden Fleece, Medea's father the king said no. He said no and Jason didn't stop asking. He said no again and again, Jason didn't stop. Finally the king said okay fine, here are three trials, but the trials were too hard. Jason came to Medea for help and Medea said no and she said no again, but Jason didn't stop and again she said no. Her will was strong. But then Eros shot her with his magic love-poisoned arrow and Medea fell in love with Jason.

But it wasn't real love and Medea knew it wasn't real. She knew it wasn't real because when she looked out her window to the forest of conifers beyond her kingdom she remembered creeping there among the trees and lying beneath the bending groaning branches and the spiraling stars and the aching moon and she remembered the magic in her bones and in her blood and she remembered that she was a witch. And when she remembered she screamed because she wanted so badly to go back to the forest, but she only screamed in her head.

She had no will, she had no control, something else somebody else controlled her body. It was Eros and his wicked spell and Medea screamed in her head and if she could have she would have killed her own self because she wasn't hers anymore, she was Jason's. But she couldn't, she couldn't kill herself, so she only screamed in her head.

Even though she was a princess, even though she was a witch, even though she was a goddess, Eros's magic was too strong. And so she helped Jason and she helped and she helped him and she helped him again. He proved himself worthy of the fleece, only it was fake because he wasn't worthy. And then he had the fleece. And then he told Medea to kill her brother, her own brother, and to butcher his body and spread his bloody butchered limbs all across her kingdom. She screamed in her head but she did it anyway because she had to because she was Jason's. Eros gave her to him.

Her father the king looked and looked for her brother and while he looked Jason escaped. He brought Medea with him because she was still useful because after all she was a princess and a goddess and a witch. They came to the kingdom of Corinth, triumphant and in-fake-love. And he vowed to love Medea forever and so she bore him two sons and for a while all was well.

But then Jason fell in love with a princess of Corinth and Medea found out. After everything she did for him. After everything she lost for him. And she couldn't kill herself because she wasn't hers she was Jason's and she couldn't kill Jason because she was his Eros gave her to him.

And so she killed their sons. And she screamed and she screamed and she screamed in her head.

Seventeen

TELL AN ADULT they always say. If something bad happens tell an adult. Tell a trusted adult. What about when there are no trusted adults? I don't even have parents really. I just have a mess. I just have the damage they've done.

From here I can see into Poppy's house. The curtains are open. They always are. At night the windows glow yellow and warm and I can see all the normal things Poppy and Willow do. Puzzles and movie nights and baking pie together and then eating it sitting at the dining room table. Normal things that are bewildering to me. I can see Willow now, a dark shape wavering behind the glass. She's moving around in the kitchen. She has the kettle in her hand. She's making tea.

But I don't feel like I can go there.

Not after Poppy left. Not after she didn't call me or text me or talk to me. Not after she finally did call me but only to ask me, accuse me, chastise me, hang up on me, reject me.

I think about knocking on the door.

I think about asking Willow can I come in and can we talk.

I think about sitting at the butcher block island that is slashed and stained with a thousand dinners and saying the words.

Just say the words, Poppy said.

I think about saying the words.

This dread is like something heavy and boneless on my chest.

And I can't. I just can't.

I knock on a different door and Suzanna, Ro's mom, answers.

"Ramona isn't here," she says.

I edge in the door and she steps back, letting me in all the way.

"Is everything okay, Virginia?" she asks.

I still don't say anything.

"I think maybe everything is not okay," Suzanna says.

She waits because she knows she's right. Things are not okay and I'm here to talk about it. "Do you want something to drink? A snack? I just picked up the most beautiful plums at the market. Why don't you sit down and I'll go make us a snack."

I sit on the couch and wedge my hands under my butt. There's a click and static and then a saxophone comes lamenting through the air, quiet though, it's quiet. Suzanna sets a tray on the coffee table. A green glass bottle of sparkling mineral water. A bowl of ripe purple plums that glow yellow from within. A small dish of gummy candy shaped like stars, green, white, red. I take one and bite into it. It tastes green, like basil, like lime.

"So," she prompts, "what did you want to tell me?"

"There is somebody who—" I start and stop and push my fist against my mouth and swallow the candy.

Suzanna doesn't say anything.

"I'm worried about this person. This girl I tutor."

"Okay," she says.

"I think maybe somebody wants to . . . I think there is a person. Her soccer coach. He, I think He might be, like, grooming her, for . . ." I take a deep shuddering breath in and then breathe out a kind of weepy groan and Suzanna gives me a look of such sympathy that I bite my bottom lip to keep from crying.

"There's a young girl who you tutor, who you're concerned somebody is grooming? For abuse?" she says.

I nod. "Yes."

"Why do you think that?" she says.

I open my mouth and then I stop. Of course she wants to know why. But I can't. I can't.

"Virginia?" she says.

My phone starts buzzing. It's Ro. I stand up. "Hello?" I say, phone to my ear.

"Hey," Ro says.

"I have to go," I say to Suzanna, seizing on the excuse because I can't tell her why.

"What's up?" I say to Ro.

Suzanna stands up too. "Virginia, wait."

But I'm already out the door jogging down the front walk, my sandals slapping on the pavement.

"Where are you?" Ro says. "Was that my mom?"

"Virginia!" Suzanna is standing on the porch.

"Virginia?" Ro says.

"The park. Come meet me," I say.

Ro must hear something in my voice. "Okay, I'm on my way," she says.

As soon as we hang up, my phone is buzzing. It's Suzanna. And then it's Suzanna again. I walk the long way to the reservoir park to give me a few minutes to compose myself. My phone goes quiet and then it buzzes. Suzanna again.

In the dark it is hard to find Ro. I stand in the warm night and scan the indistinct field for her. A car cruises by, music thumping, black windows up.

Ro is twirling on the tire swing. She pauses long enough for me to slip my legs in beside hers and then we start spinning again, this way and that, in the dappled streetlight shadows beneath the ponderosa pine. "Why were you with my mom?" Ro says.

But then she pulls her buzzing phone out of her pocket. "Hey," she says, sounding not cold but maybe reserved. "I'm not home. I'm at the reservoir park. I'm with Virginia. Okay. I guess."

I give her a look but she doesn't see. She's looking at the road. And then Hannah pulls up in a shiny silver Subaru and falls out of the car, crying and shivering and calling Ro's name.

"I told them," Hannah says. "I told them I love you." She stops and weeps and wipes her face and says, "I love you. I do."

Ro rushes to Hannah and they tangle their arms around each other and Hannah cries into her neck and Ro runs her hands through Hannah's hair murmuring, "I love you too, baby, I love you too."

But Hannah keeps going. "They said they won't pay for college anymore but I don't care. It doesn't matter. I just need to be with you. I love you," she says to Ro, looking at Ro's face like she can't believe the beauty of it, the beauty of Ro, her soul, her whole entire self.

And as Hannah relaxes into Ro's embrace and as her tears dry and her gasping breath slows, I realize maybe just being with Ramona, listening to her voice, being in her arms, is enough.

Eighteen

HANNAH AND RO linger in their love. I know it shouldn't but it hurts to watch them. Everything. Just everything. Everything is beautiful for Ro. Everything is falling to pieces for me.

I need to go. Where can I go? I need to just go. I open my mouth to say something but I don't know what and then I'm interrupted by a car door slamming and a discordant burst of laughter. We all turn toward the road. It's Brooke and Edison and Isaiah and Rand.

"Fuck," Ro says, looking annoyed.

Fuck.

Ro shakes out her hair and straightens her shoulders, composing herself. Hannah latches her hand securely in Ro's and I can tell she wants to make sure everybody can see. Ro is Hannah's. Hannah is Ro's. It's a declaration. I lean back in my swing and wish for some kind of substance to dull the sharp pain in my chest.

"Hey!" Brooke runs over. She jumps on a swing and kicks hard, swinging to and fro, her short skirt sailing, her round thighs showing. Ro grimaces and the boys make their way over. Rand is rapping the song that came out today. Ro shakes her head laughing and shouts at Rand to shut up. The laughter and shit-talking and gossip swell around me and I close my eyes and push my swing with my feet and wait.

"Virginia, come help me with this thing," Edison says. Rand grins at him. "In my car," Edison says, and Isaiah laughs.

I feel Ro's eyes on me. Brooke is shrieking about something on her phone, not paying attention, and she shows it to Rand, who looks down her shirt while pretending to look at her phone, and I have a brief reprieve. I shake my head at Edison. He's staring at me like he can't believe it and then his phone buzzes.

He reads the message and rolls his eyes and says, "Well, fuck you too."

"Are you still beefing?" Rand asks.

Brooke's ears perk and twitch like a dog listening to a rabbit in the underbrush. "What's going on?"

Edison doesn't respond to her.

Rand says, "Sweet piece like that, I wouldn't be complaining."

Edison grins and lights a cigarette.

"What, you and Thalia?" Brooke says.

Edison has a predatory look. It might be about Brooke, who has silky wheat-colored hair and an itty-bitty waist, or it could be about me. "We might call it quits."

"No!" Brooke's cornflower eyes are round.

Edison shrugs. "I have to give other girls a chance to play. Right, Virginia?"

There's a pause.

He thumbs over his shoulder, pointing at his car. "I mean, you want to?"

No. No. No. No, I don't want to. The words bubble up in my mouth like a burp and bulge against my lips trying to emerge like a spindly debutant ready for her coming out party.

Brooke whips her head back and forth between Edison and me.

"You know what, Virginia? Never mind. I'm good. You're like a fucking couch, you know? You're a fucking Stacy. Sorry for tossing you a few pity fucks, but I'm done trying."

"What the fuck?" Ro stands up. "You're such a fucking prick." She gets in Edison's face and it occurs to me how tall she is. There is less than an inch difference between her and Edison.

He backs away but he doesn't look alarmed. He looks smug. "She threw the ball, I caught it."

I press my fingertips into my forehead and close my eyes. As if it were all just me.

"Oh my god," Brooke says. "What's going on?"

"Mind your own fucking business," Ro snaps at her. She grabs my hand and drags me away and Hannah follows. Behind us I can hear Edison and Rand laughing, Isaiah going "Damn," and Brooke saying "What?" over and over again.

Ro deposits me into the passenger seat. I look at Ro and she looks back at me, the fury fading and sadness filling her eyes. "Virginia, what was Edison talking about?"

"It wasn't my fault" is the only thing I can think to say.

Ro stares at her steering wheel for a second. "Did he, like . . . what happened between you guys?"

"It wasn't my fault," I say again stupidly.

Hannah is in the back seat.

"You can tell me," Ro says.

"I can't even say it," I say.

"But are you okay?" she says like she's not ready to give up yet.

I shake my head. It's only a matter of time. Before everybody knows. Before Thalia knows.

As though there is some reprieve in my broken unpunctuated texts, I'm trying to explain. As though I can possibly explain why I did it. Why I've done any of the things I've done.

im sorry

i know it doesnt matter

that im saying sorry

i know it doesnt matter that im sorry

i know it doesnt help

but i am

My thumbs are poised and I'm trying to come up with words. The right words. The ones that will maybe not absolve but at least illuminate. As if providing understanding could change anything. My phone pings with an answer.

Stop texting me.

Thalia always uses proper punctuation.

· · ·

I don't care that it's nine in the morning. They've already started, so why shouldn't I? I wipe the wine off my lips and take another drink.

"Fuck!" I spit a wet glob onto the floor. It's a moth, stained crimson by the wine it drowned in. I shouldn't have left it uncorked last night, but where was my brain? Drowning in wine like the moth.

They're screaming names at each other.

"Wankstain!"

That's a new one. Mom must be reading those British crime novels she loves.

"Cunt!"

No originality.

I press my eyeball to the neck of the wine bottle looking for more dead insects.

"Go fuck yourself, you fucking asshole!"

I can't see any, so I drink some more.

There's a crash and a wail. It sounds like my mom's putting it on for attention. I doubt she's actually hurt. She just wants my dad to think she is. To turn around and say, "Oh my god I never meant to hurt you!" But he doesn't. He slams the door to the garage and peels out, screeching his tires like a wankstain.

She stops wailing as soon as he's gone.

I'm not doing it.

I'm not going down there and comforting her.

I grab shorts off the floor, pull a tank top over my head, shove my feet into the nearest flip-flops, find my big bag that I can fit a book and a few bottles into.

She starts crying and I hesitate at the window.

No.

I'm not doing it.

I pop out my screen. It's mangled from years of abuse.

I drop.

I know I look like shit. I haven't washed my hair in a decade. I fell asleep with my makeup on last night and now it's smeared all down my face.

I jog down the sidewalk, trying to get away from my house as quickly as possible.

Where do I go?

I can't call Poppy. She's angry, she can't deal with me, she's sick of me, sick of my shit, sick of my licentious ways. And she probably wouldn't answer anyway. Paz is on team Thalia. She has to be. I know she loves me, but how can she stand by me now? Now that it's out. Really definitely out.

What a slut I am.

I stop and stand on the street corner. I call Ro. She doesn't pick up. I call her again. She doesn't pick up. Her house is dark and gray in the rain.

It's wet and windy and cold. A car swishes by and splashes

puddle water on my feet. I stand there and stare at my phone.

I have four missed calls from Suzanna and seven unread texts.

I breathe.

I put my phone in my bag.

I scratch a mosquito bite on my ankle.

I start walking again.

I walk.

I jog for a little while.

I stop and take a drink of wine.

I put the bottle back in my bag and walk some more.

Eventually, I can't avoid the question anymore.

What now?

I turn and start walking in a different direction. There are goose bumps on my skin, and my feet are wet and dirty from puddles and I am shivering.

I pass Poppy's house.

I pass Ro's.

Paz's.

And now I'm here. I can't knock. I can't go in.

Like a lovesick teenage boy, I throw pebbles at her window.

. . .

I don't know why I came here. I don't know what I'm going to say. I don't know where to go or what to do or what to say or who to be. I just know this is where it started. This is where my story began.

Thalia stands at her window. The contempt in her eyes takes my breath away. She disappears and I turn, trying to figure out where to go from here, but then I hear the front door open and close and she is standing in front of me with red eyes and tear-stained skin and exhausted shoulders and slept-on hair. She looks like me. Like I am looking at a reflection of my weathered derelict self.

"I'm sorry," I say.

"You're a bad person, Virginia," Thalia says.
    "I know." I feel my heart droop like a rotten fruit.
    This is what I came for.
    "I know," I say again.
    A heady sweet fruit, ruptured and falling and bursting. Fermenting. My heart is like vinegar.
    I turn and leave this space that Thalia occupies. Breathing her air, I feel like my lungs will collapse in shame.
    I am unaware of the transition between leaving walking

running and suddenly the pavement is streaking beneath me, gum and cracks blurring into wavering streamers.

This body.

I stumble and stop, clutching my stomach.

No matter how fast I run, I can never run away from this ruined body.

Thalia's words chase me, biting at my heels. I land at home but my heartbeat is brief and heavy and I know I can't stay here.

I have no sanctuary. I have nowhere to go.

My thoughts burn.

I stumble to Ravenna Park, far enough away, big enough, wet enough, empty enough on a day like this.

It is quiet now and the cold settles in and the rain starts and the woods are wet and green and I start to hear the sounds, the ones that lie beneath the cars and music and chatter. I am suddenly, sharply aware of the implications of my solitude and the things I've gathered.

Gin, rum, tequila, three bottles almost full, weed, a bottle of extra-strength Tylenol, some assorted prescriptions.

I think of the creek close by, down a sloping muddy hill. I think of its face, flowing and swift. I think of my face, blue and still, beneath the surface. I think of giving the water a kiss.

I sink more and more into the sting and burn and things start to churn and my chin is salty with tears. The tequila sears down my throat and I remember shots and salacious dancing, shimmying and flirting and getting at least a little bit naked.

I lift the bottle end over end and it goes down

and

down

and

down

until I am slippery and I think I might slip into a salty coma
and I think I might like it and it might be quite nice to be on ice
so I can while away some of this painful life,

down

and

down

until I am content with this pain.

I emerge a ghost. But I always was. Ever since. I am a little girl
ghost. I haunt this body. I don't own it. I don't even want it. I just
reside in it, a revenant.

I am still drunk and gray as I walk home in the dark. I stum-
ble into the street and a truck blares its horn at me. I'm angry.
I'm destructive. I'm devastated. I'm at the edge. I'm at the end.
There is nowhere to go from here.

I drink as I text, searching, and finally an answer. Party at
Isaiah's.

· · ·

I'm so drunk, they all stare, Thalia, Edison, Rumi, and fucking Liz. Fuck you, fuck you, and fuck you too. Rumi is not happy that I'm here. I laugh like I don't give a fuck.

I.

Don't.

Give.

A.

Fuck.

The staccato words vibrate on my teeth and I wash them down with liquor.

I am passed out, passing out. Black is the world, gray fading to black, gray and blue and bleeding purple.

I feel an arm around my shoulders and my head lolls against somebody's hand. It is so heavy. The room sways.

Giggling. "Take a picture."

"She's so fucked up."

Thalia laughs. I feel a hand on my bare leg and I can't manage to pry my eyes open or lift my head.

The sensation of skin on skin fades.

Now there is something cold. Cold and wet and creeping up my thigh. A pen. On my legs.

More laughter.

Bodies pressing against me. A body, somebody sitting next to me, jostling me, picks up my arm, holds my wrist, my hand flopping, I can feel it but I can't stop it, and drops it again, my arm slaps against my bare leg like meat, like a cut of raw meat.

I can't move. But part of me welcomes the darkness. This small death.

My story ends with this.

But now there is angry noise.

In my myth Ro comes in with a blazing light. She radiates anger. She is so beautiful in her power, her strength.

In this story she grabs Liz by the neck and throws her from me onto the floor. When Thalia starts to shout at her Ro strikes her across the face and Thalia falls. "You should be ashamed of yourself!"

In my myth Ro has wings and fire. She is the archetypal hero.

She pulls me up, guides my stumbling legs.

Rumi's face is white, shocked, pained, weak.

"Coward," she spits at him.

Her rage is a wildfire, burning through my stupor. She throws me into the seat of her car. Out of control, she tears into the night-shrouded street.

"How could you be so careless?" she screams at me.

"Virginia!"

I can barely lift my head.

"Virginia!"

nothing there is nothing here just nothing

. . .

There is some passage of time. Salty tears, acidic vomit, mixed with pools of nothingness. I try to pass out on the sidewalk of some road but Ro won't let me. She drags me back into the car and eventually into the bliss of a soft bed.

Medea comes to me in my sleep. She comes to me cloaked in her whole entire story. The beginning and the middle and the end. The terrible thousands-of-years-long ending that is horrifying, unspeakable, that I hate. I dream it, all of it.

Medea comes to me. She comes to me cloaked in her whole entire story. But we already know her story, don't we? No, she whispers on the back of my neck, no you don't.

Once upon a time there was this beautiful woman who was also a princess who was also a goddess who was also a witch. An evil witch, right? Because she killed her kids, right? No, she whispers, no.

When Jason came, she said no and Eros cast a spell on her and she fell in love with Jason. Real love? Magic love? Fake love? All of the above? Who knows, it was a spell and it was three thousand years ago. Who knows? How can we possibly think we actually know when something happened three thousand years ago? (Maybe it was longer than that, we don't actually know.) You don't know, she whispers, you don't actually know.

(But we think we know.) We think we know that she fell in some kind of love with Jason and so for Jason she did horrible things (because she was the archetypal helper maiden who belongs to our stories). She even killed her two sons, right? Because Jason left her for some other woman, right? She took revenge on Jason by killing their two sons because she was an evil witch of a woman who cared more about her pride and her vanity and getting her own way than anything, even her two beautiful, innocent sons (evil witch), at least that's what people say, right? No! she screams. No! That's just a story!

Because before she had two sons they say she had three sons or they say she had one son and one daughter but now they've decided it's actually definitely really two sons. And in some stories she's not a goddess, she's a mortal. And in some stories she is the daughter of an Oceanid, an ocean nymph, a child of the titans. But now they've definitely decided she's just a wicked evil witch with lots of ambition.

And sometimes they say Medea killed her brother and then they say that she cut up his body and spread his bloody butchered limbs all over (evil witch). But in some stories it's Jason who killed her brother but now they've decided it works better if Medea does it and she does it bloody and brutal because she's an evil witch, right? Because only an evil witch would kill her own children.

But in one story they tell it like this: After Jason left Medea for the princess of Corinth, Medea buried her two beautiful, innocent sons in the earth of the temple of Hera because she believed this would make her two beautiful, innocent sons immortal. But she was wrong and they died and it was horrible that they died and

Medea never forgave herself and she grieved until the end of her days because she was wrong and they were dead.

And in another story they tell it like this: After Jason left Medea for the princess of Corinth, Medea lamented to the women of Corinth. Yes, she whispers in my ear, this.

She said listen: I was put under a spell and I fell in-fake-love and I helped Jason. When he needed to kill the never-sleeping dragon, I killed the never-sleeping dragon. When he needed to resist fire, I gave him a salve. When he fought dragon-tooth skeletons, I told him how to trick them. When he needed to distract my father, I watched him kill my brother and then I took the blame. When he fled, I followed. I left my home, my family. I live in a land where I am a barbarian, an evil witch. And now he has left me for your princess and so I killed her and her father the king with poisoned gold. I mock Jason for his great gilded dreams and for his fickle treachery.

Medea tells this story, this lament, to the women of Corinth. Can't they understand?

No, she whispers, they couldn't.

They killed her children because she killed their princess and their king. Because Medea was an evil witch. And *that was the last time Medea told her own story. After that it became somebody else's story. Hesiod told her story. Eumelus told her story. Pausanias told her story. Pindar told her story. Creophylus told her story. And then Euripides told her story.*

And when Euripides told her story, he made her a child murderer. He made her murder her own children. And from then on forever more they whispered her name. They said: Medea killed her own children. Forever, that's what they said. Forever! she screams. And she screams and she screams and she screams in my head.

Nineteen

I WAKE UP even though I don't want to. The ceiling is white and cracked. I remember a Madeline book that I owned a million years ago. She was in the hospital and would lie in bed staring at the ceiling. There was a crack shaped like a bunny.

These cracks have no shape. They are aimless and stained with brown water.

I wish I wasn't here. I wish I wasn't anywhere.

How many mornings have I woken up like this? Hungover and ashamed. Wishing I could sleep forever so I would never have to face the poor decisions I made the night before.

The door swings open and Ro comes into the room, Rita May trundling behind her. She's showered and dressed and functional in a way that is entirely foreign to me. "I'm sorry I got so angry at you last night." She sits on the end of the bed clutching a cup of tea.

"It's okay."

"No, it's not." She hands me the tea and I sit up and take a drink. "It's not your fault, what happened. It was them, Edison and Thalia and all those pieces of shit who stood by and watched like what was happening wasn't a big deal. Like it was funny. It's their fault."

There is writing on my thigh in bleeding black marker. I trace it with a finger. *Slut. Whore. Fucking slag. Enter here*, with an arrow pointing at my vagina ending at my underwear line.

"Virginia."

"What?"

"What's going on with you?"

My stomach rolls. "What do you mean?"

"I talked to my mom."

I don't say anything.

"She told me there's somebody you're worried about."

My mouth fills with bile.

"That there's a little girl you think might be, like, being abused."

I lurch off the bed and run for the bathroom down the hallway, ricocheting off the walls. Ro stands behind me for a minute and then kneels next to me, her hand on my back, other hand on my forehead, as I throw up. She hands me a glass of water when I sit back against the wall, then a towel, which I press to my face and then she just looks at me and waits.

"I can't right now, Ro," I say, and I don't think I've ever felt so broken. "I just can't."

"Okay," she says.

She leads me back to bed and I sleep all day. I wake up and Ro is watching a serial killer documentary on her laptop. I wake up again and Ro is lying next to me reading a paperback. I wake up again and she is texting and giggling and I ask her and she says it's Hannah with a small private smile on her face.

I fall back asleep until the room is dim and golden with the sunset and Suzanna comes in with a plate and bottles of bubbly water. Her makeup is off and she's wearing a robe and her hair is wrapped in silk. Her face is always beautiful, but there's something about the yellow silk framing her brown skin and her bare lips that make almost a perfect circle. Sometimes her beauty just stuns me.

"I know you're sick, baby, but you need to eat a little something," she says, sitting by my feet.

Ramona is lying next to me scrolling through her phone. "She's not sick, she's hungover."

"You hush," Suzanna says, and Ro sticks her tongue out without looking away from her phone.

Suzanna hands me the plate. It's toast and blackberry jam. "My own," she says.

"What?"

"We made the jam, right, love?" she says to Ro.

Ro says to me, "Right, so you better eat it," and I smile for the first time all day.

Today Suzanna is too worried and too kind, but I know it won't last. Once, even though we wedged a towel under the door, she could smell weed coming out of Ro's room and I don't think I've ever felt so guilty for getting high. She made me feel like it was immoral and I was betraying my own body, my own self. I know what she's going to say about me drinking so much. It's not safe. What if something had happened to me? I'm poisoning my body. It's self-destructive.

I know it's self-destructive. That's why I do it.

Suzanna leaves with the plate and Ro puts her phone away and rolls to face me. "Virginia," she says.

I close my eyes. "I know."

"You have to tell me."

"I know," I say again.

"Who is it? That you're worried about? Is it Rumi's little sister?"

I nod with my eyes still closed.

Ro touches my cheek. "Tell me."

*O*nce upon a time there was this little girl. She lived in a house in the woods with her stepmother and stepfather. Her stepfather was often away and when he was home he was cruel. The stepmother was a selfish, petty woman and she cared little for the girl.

One day the little girl woke up and the house was empty. She was scared. She worried that without somebody there to protect her something bad would happen. And something bad did happen. A man, no a wolf, no a monster, no a beast, came into her house where she was supposed to be safe. And He touched her and hurt her and cut open her body and ate away at her insides until her body was hollow and dead and the little girl was a ghost.

When her parents, no I mean her stepparents, came home they didn't notice. They sat with the beast at their table and they shared their dinner with Him while the little girl-ghost watched from a shadow. And it was like she never even existed at all.

They weren't really her stepparents, but you already knew that, didn't you? It doesn't make sense to have two stepparents who are married to each other. They were the girl's real mother and real father. And her father was often away and he was often cruel and her mother was *selfish and petty and the girl was alone figuratively and literally. She woke up and there was a monster, a beast, a wolf, but He was also a man and He touched her and hurt her and hollowed her out and He and her parents were friends and they stayed friends.*

Even after. Ever since.

And I've been standing in a shadow, watching, ever since.

Twenty

THE FIRST TIME He came over I was so excited.

I waited at the door, eager to see Him coming. We all laughed. I was giddy. I helped make dinner. This great friend of mine, this person with whom I had shared so many secrets, He utterly charmed my parents. He helped my mom wash the dishes. He stood on the back porch with my dad and drank bourbon. He decided to stay and play poker with my dad and they called over some more friends and I was sent to bed.

I fell asleep happy listening to my friend and my dad laugh as if He could maybe possibly influence my shitty abusive father. Maybe He could make my dad a little bit like Him. Kind. Attentive. Interested in me.

He and I, we would hang out and talk. I told Him about my dad and mom and how they drank and fought and how they ignored me and how sometimes my dad would get mean. I told Him more about that than anyone ever before. He said He wanted to get to know them better.

I don't know what I thought. I thought maybe He wanted to protect me.

. . .

I was dreaming when my door swung open and a bright light fell on my face. What was I dreaming? I don't remember, honestly. It was washed away in the wake of what happened.

So. The door opened and the light hit my eyes. I squinted, already alarmed. I'd been dragged out of bed in the middle of the night before. But it wasn't my dad coming to make me pay for some infraction. It was Him. His bare feet padded across the thick carpet and I closed my eyes, turning onto my side and pretending I was asleep.

I was nervous. A little excited. I thought He might be about to invite me on an adventure or to sneak me a chocolate bar or a bag of popcorn before He went home. The house was quiet and I figured that my mom had gone to bed and my dad was passed out drunk.

He climbed into bed behind me.

He pulled my body into His. Then He put His hand up my shirt and cupped my tiny eleven-year-old breast. He breathed into my neck and His breath smelled like alcohol. He pushed His hips into my butt and soon He had an erection. I pretended to sleep while He held me and smelled my neck and stroked my torso.

That night that was it. He fell asleep and I didn't move. He rolled away from me and started snoring. I still didn't move. I didn't move until my mom walked past my open door in the morning and laughed about how He had been so drunk the night before He passed out in my bed.

We sat at the kitchen table and He joked with my mom and

drank coffee and threw wadded-up paper towels at my dad's prone form and He winked at me while I ate my Lucky Charms.

I smiled at Him because I wanted to reassure Him that everything was okay.

"We have to tell somebody," Ro says.

"I know."

"Like, now."

So Ro and I sit on the floor, and Suzanna in her robe and Noah still in his tie with little teal cat faces on it, they sit on the couch.

"Virginia is worried that Rumi's little sister is being groomed for abuse," Ro says. She squeezes my hand like, *There, okay, it's okay now,* but it's not because now I need to explain why.

Noah takes a deep breath and I can tell he's trying to keep his voice low and calm for me when he says, "Why do you think that, Virginia?"

I look at Suzanna, fiddling with the silk tie of her robe. She smiles at me but the corners of her lips tremble.

Noah doesn't make me nervous, but as Ro tightens her grip on my hand and looks at me expectantly, I feel like I can't see like there are a million tiny yellow spots clouding my eyes like my lungs are collapsing like a pillow is pressed to my ears my face my mouth my eyes like I can't see like I'm panicking.

. . .

it hurts

my chest hurts

"My chest hurts."

it's like static

it's like noise

like I'm going to throw up again

like my throat is choked is thick

"I feel like I'm going to throw up!"

it's like noise in my head

"I can't see! I can't hear!"

like fuzz

like static

and crashing waves

and white noise

"Virginia!" Ro's voice is far away.

noise

"Mom!" she yells.

noise

Suddenly Suzanna's face is in my face, her hands on my shoulders. "Look at me, baby," she is saying. "Look at my eyes."

noise

My face is tingling and my eyes are bouncing around and I can't focus and I still can't catch my breath and it hurts my chest hurts!

I'm gasping

"What is your name?" Suzanna says.

trying to breathe

"Virginia," I gasp.

noise

"How many legs do you have?" Her hands on my shoulders, her face right in front of mine.

breathe

"Two."

gasp

"How many hands do you have?"

clutch my chest it hurts my chest it hurts

"Two."

breathe

"How many fingers do you have?"

slower

"Ten."

slow

"What color are your eyes?"

slow

"Blue."

"What is your middle name?"

"Katherine."

"What is my name?"

"Suzanna."

"Who am I?"

"Ro's mom."

"Where is Ramona?"

Ro is standing in the corner crying. "She's right there." I point.

"Where are you?"

"Right here."

"That's right, Virginia. You're right here. You're safe. You're safe here with us."

Suzanna's hands are steady on my shoulders. She is strong and she is capable and she is wise and she is kind and I already knew all these things about her but now I see that she is also determined to help me.

Suddenly I feel small and young like an eleven-year-old who doesn't know how to protect herself. I bend over and crumple and I am crying so hard, I feel like I can't catch my breath. Suzanna's hands are on my back and she is telling me it's okay it's okay it's okay just cry you're safe just cry you're safe it's okay Virginia it's okay it's okay it's okay you're safe here you're safe here.

I'm safe here.

I have to say the words. I have to say the name. I have to say His name.

Somehow I have to say it.

"The reason why," I say, and I take a deep breath. And another. I am so afraid of being overcome with panic again.

Ro and Suzanna and Noah, they're all watching me. I see my fear reflected in their faces, suppressed like they are trying to be calm for me.

"What happened was . . ." I press my hands to my face.

I have to say it.

Where do I start?

It's the way Lyra smiles at Him, all hopeful eyes and stretchy lips that show too many teeth and too much need. It's the way He smiles back at her, like she's a puzzle He's assembling and He's getting to the last couple pieces and soon it will be done.

It's their outings, their private dates, their secret time.

It's the mood ring, claiming her, naming her His, chafing at her finger, the way it chafed at mine. The way it marked me His victim, it marks Lyra.

I have to do this. I have to be brave.

"The reason why I think Lyra is being groomed by somebody is . . ."

Suzanna nods reassuringly.

"The same person abused me." And then Ro is sitting right in front of me so I'm only looking at her face and her eyes are filled with tears and she's holding both my hands in hers and saying "It's okay, keep talking," because I need to get past this moment. I need to tell them about Lyra. I need to tell them who it is.

"The person who abused me." I pause and close my eyes, His face swimming before me, smiling kind confident with people who love Him and people who believe in Him and people who trust Him.

I open my eyes. "It was Thalia's dad."

(I can't even say his name.)

*O*nce upon a time there was this beautiful goddess. Her name was Oshun. She was the goddess of love and lust and beauty and youth. Her beauty was a gift to her people. Her beauty was like ripples in the water. She lived on the delta in the mangrove swamps where the birds came unbidden, the spoonbill and the ibis and the heron and the cormorant, and she lived in the grasses that grew after the floods and caught catfish that swam lazy through the waters and ate the sweet mangoes and avocados that grew on fruit trees. Oshun loved her home more than anything. More than her beauty and more than the people who loved her beautiful self, she loved her home the most.

But then Olodumare, the king of all the gods, became angry and he withheld the rains. The rivers shrank and the grasses died and the fruit dried and the birds flew away and they didn't come back. Oshun wept and she beat her fists upon the sun-baked riverbed until they were bloody and she vowed to bring back the rains no matter what it cost her. But Olodumare was so high up in the sky, even the birds couldn't find him.

The older gods, like teasing brothers and sisters, said she was just beautiful and not powerful and they said she could never do it. But she knew she could do it. So she turned herself into a peacock, the most beautiful *of all the birds, and up and up and up she flew into the bluest part of the sky and when her body became tired she kept flying and when it became hard to breathe she kept flying and when her feathers fell out one by one she kept flying. All that mattered was her delta and her birds.*

When she reached Olodumare, she had struggled so hard and for so long that she was as bald and withered and exhausted as a vulture. Olodumare nursed her back to health and he told her that he was so moved by her sacrifice and her power that he would bring back the rains.

She wasn't beautiful anymore. She looked at her reflection in the flowing waters of the delta and she didn't recognize herself. But as the birds flew back one by one, the heron and the ibis and the spoonbill and the cormorant, and the grasses waved in the saltwater breeze and as she drank the sweet juice of the mangoes, it didn't matter. She had saved her home. She thought she wasn't beautiful, but she was. She was the most beautiful, the most powerful woman in the world. And she lived happily ever after. At least that's my guess.

Twenty-one

SUZANNA SAYS WE have to report it. That's the best way to protect Lyra. She says things about Child Protective Services, about how the police will probably arrest him and about how he'll probably post bail. She says things about hearings and statutes of limitations and defense lawyers and prosecuting attorneys. It's hard to listen. It's hard to not cover my ears with my hands like a little girl and scream for her to stop just stop.

Suzanna questions me and makes phone calls and we sit in the living room and Ro drifts in and out, restless, wandering, picking up a book and putting it down, opening and closing the fridge. Suzanna murmurs to her and Ro makes us cinnamon toast and iced honey-and-mint tea and brings plates of strawberries and sliced mangoes and tiny sweet grapes.

Ro nibbles on her toast and compulsively scrolls through her phone and picks it up and puts it down again and again. After a while she puts her headphones on and stands at the kitchen window and stares out while she listens to a podcast. Probably that one about the French Revolution she's been into lately.

At the end of it all, at the end of the day, Suzanna puts her arm around me. "I asked Noah to get takeout," she says. "I am so tired of making dinner. All that planning and shopping and making sure we use the ingredients we already have so we don't waste food. I could stop doing that forever and be just fine. He's going to stop on the way home. What are you in the mood for?"

I shrug.

"What about that Vietnamese place? We could get bánh mi?" Ro says, taking off her headphones.

I look from Ro to Suzanna, both smiling at me encouragingly like they just want to make everything okay, a little bit more okay, with delicious fresh food.

"Sure," I say, and reach for Ro's hand. "Can I have the tofu, please?"

Suzanna nods and reaches for her phone.

"Thank you," I say. For dinner. For letting me stay here. For keeping me safe.

Suzanna looks at me and for a second it seems like she wants to cry. She tugs at her gold hoop earring and then smiles again, as bright and cheerful as I think she can make it. "Of course, baby."

After dinner Ro and me go to bed even though it's still light out. She opens the window to let the AC out and the warm sweet air in and we share her pillow and watch reruns on her laptop. Rita May trundles panting into the room. Ro doesn't move until the dog jumps up onto the bed and puts her head on Ro's leg, wedging herself between our bodies. Ro reaches down and rests her hand on Rita May's head. She checks her phone again and smiles and groans and throws it across the room. It lands faceup and glimmers in the lamplight.

I watch her and smile too. "I'm so glad you're happy. I'm so glad Hannah stepped up."

Ro closes her eyes and presses a hand to her mouth like she's trying to smother her smile. "I'm happy too. It's too much. Like, how do I process these positive emotions?" She laughs and wiggles her shoulders and shakes her head like she's crazy, sticking her tongue out, and then puts a pillow over her face and shrieks into it. Rita May lifts her head up and looks over her shoulder at Ro, panting. I smile small, watching her. I can't match her energy, but I wrap my hand around her wrist and squeeze.

She looks over at me and the smile drops off her face. "Want to talk about it?" she says.

"How bad is it going to be?" I say. "When it gets out about Thalia's dad? Because it will."

Ro pulls away and nods. "A lot of people aren't going to believe you."

"After the first time it happened I tried to forget it. I thought maybe he was just drunk and I don't know, thought I was Thalia's mom or something. I thought maybe it was a mistake, you know? A misunderstanding. I didn't want it to be anything else. I didn't want it to be real. I didn't want it to be abuse."

Ro closes her laptop and puts it on the floor and snuggles closer to Rita May and me.

"I went over to Thalia's a day or two later. Her dad got me alone." I shiver and pull the blanket over my shoulder. "Thalia was watching TV. Thalia's mom was cleaning the kitchen. I went to Thalia's room to get my phone. He followed me. He sat down on the bed and pulled me down next to him. He took my phone out of my hands and said, 'I want to show you something.' He showed me a video of a girl giving somebody a blow job. There was this big banner across the top, BARELY LEGAL TEENS ASKING FOR IT! He kept looking at me to make sure I was watching. I remember pretending to watch but really I was staring at the banner. I don't know why I pretended to watch. Maybe I didn't want to make him mad. Maybe I didn't want to draw attention to what was happening. I didn't want Thalia or her mom to see us. And maybe I wanted to make him happy."

I pause because the next thing is worse and it's stuck in my throat.

"He said, 'Do you think that's something you can do?' About the blow job."

I can't meet Ro's eyes, so I sit up and stroke the soft silky fur of Rita May's ear. "I'm ashamed. Still. To this day. I'm ashamed of every second of the abuse. I can't shake the idea that it was my fault. If only I had done something differently. Maybe the abuse wouldn't have happened or maybe it would have stopped sooner."

Finally I look at Ro. Her cheeks are wet with tears and she still doesn't say anything.

"It's like an abyss. As soon as I start thinking about all the things I could have done."

"It's okay," she says.

"I know people aren't going to believe me. I can barely stand to believe myself."

"It's okay," Ro says again.

"It's not." I shake my head. "It's not okay, Ro."

"But it's going to be okay. It is. Eventually."

I'm ashamed and afraid and exhausted. I feel like I'm a hundred years old. I wish I drank whiskey and played guitar and then I could numb and twang and maybe that would help. Belittled and depressed and underemployed. Staring out the dingy window of an extended stay hotel, turning the blinds so I can stare at a great gray rushing freeway, dark and lit up with orange passing lights. Maybe then something would make sense.

But I'm not any of those things, so I dig my fingers into my thighs and press my hand hard into my skull and my hair is greasy and I know my dishwater roots are showing and I hate myself.

"Virginia?" Ro says.

I look up at her.

"Do you want to tell me more?"

"It was like choking on a rubber ball wedged in the back of my throat. I knew what was happening the first time he made me do it. We knew what a blow job was. Remember there was that rumor about Edison getting one from that seventh grader? I mean obviously it was so stupid and not true.

"So I knew what it was. He smiled at me. He already had an erection. My hair got twisted around his pinkie. I remember how much it hurt, my hair, how he was pulling that little piece of hair again and again. He held my head still and like . . . I kept gagging and he wouldn't stop. And then I threw up and he did stop. He got me a towel and cleaned me up and then made me finish. When he came, I threw up again."

Ramona has tears running down her face and she is gripping her mouth with her hands, covering her mouth as if to keep herself from screaming. She is horrified.

I clutch my stomach and moan. "I've never said that before," I say, and I start to cry again again again. "I haven't, I never, seeing you so horrified, it's like it makes me remember how horrifying it actually is, what actually happened." And then we're both crying, holding each other.

I remember.

Feeling like my mind was being split into pieces.

A piece that observed what my body was experiencing, the probing the wetness the hardness the pain.

A piece that observed the horror the vile the sickness the degradation of what he was doing to me of what was happening to me.

I pull away and Ro says through her tears, "Do you want to keep telling me?"

"I was afraid to embarrass him. To make him mad, to make him feel bad, to hurt his feelings. And I just wanted it to be over I just wanted to get it over with I wanted to do anything to make it be done. There were so many times, Ro. So many things I did. I'm so fucking ashamed."

"No, Virginia!" Ro says, sharp and angry. "No. You have *nothing* to be ashamed of."

"But I—"

She leans forward and presses her hands to either side of my face and I can feel her breath. "You just *can't* let yourself be ashamed."

"But I am."

"I know," she says, wiping tears from her cheeks, "I just want you to be okay."

"But I'm not okay! I don't know how to be okay. I don't know if I'll ever be okay."

"I just . . . I want to help you, Virginia, what can I do? What can I do to help you?"

"I don't know. Just don't stop loving me."

"I won't ever," she says, pulling me to her and hugging me fiercely, loving me fiercely.

Twenty-two

SEAN SAYS THALIA'S dad is a great guy. Sean's daughter Sam is in my grade at Elderberry. Sam plays soccer. When she was ten, eleven, twelve, thirteen, fourteen, he coached her.

Sean says Thalia's dad is a wonderful person. Sean says he was always professional and respectful and gracious to his daughter. Sean says the unfounded accusations against Thalia's dad are unconscionable. He says there's no way they're true. He says he doesn't know anything about me but maybe I have some kind of emotional problem. He says maybe I'm on drugs. He says he doesn't know why I would say these terrible things about Thalia's dad but he knows they're not true.

Sean says yes he would trust Thalia's dad with his own daughter any day. She nods along next to him, her dark eyes somber, like she can't imagine the depravity of somebody who would lie like I did.

It's on the local news. I watch it on Ro's bedroom floor, leaning up against her bed, the carpet making itchy imprints on my legs.

They won't say my name, the reporters. But on Instagram some people from my high school say what a slut I am. Like, I'm such a slut, if anything did happen, I probably liked it. They say look at this video. It's of the night I passed out and Thalia and them drew all over my legs. Look at this video of the drunk slut. I watch it on my phone. I watch again and again while I sit on the toilet pretending to shit. The image wavers along my sprawled open legs up to where you can see a sliver of my purple underwear and where the arrow points to my vagina saying *Enter Here* and then it skitters over my head lolling back on the couch and my eyes are slits and it pans over to where Thalia is laughing and Edison is dead-eyed and behind the camera somebody says to pour some beer on my tits and Thalia pretends to but then she says it's a waste of good beer and drinks it instead and then it's over and I watch it again. And then I scroll through the comments and people say how they want to enter there and they say how I'm asking for it and they say how somebody should teach me a lesson by ass-raping me while I'm passed out drunk like some kind of street rat hooker.

And then Ro pounds on the door and she says she saw it and I need to stop watching it and she's going to get Instagram to take it down because it's harassment.

They talk about my body like it's not mine. The comments. The messages I start getting. They say I'm disgusting for strutting around wearing my body thinking I'm hot and dressing like a whore and who do I think I am? They say I probably liked it, what Thalia's dad did. They say I act like I have a right to say no to sex but obviously I'm such a slut, if I ever say no, they say it's only because I'm just being a cock-tease-whore-bitch-prude.

They talk about my body like it belongs to whoever wants to fuck it.

They talk about me like they want to fuck me and then beat the shit out of me and then fuck me some more and then leave me bleeding and bruised with a broken face and then maybe I won't think I'm so hot. Then maybe I won't think I'm too good. Then maybe I won't think so much of myself.

They talk about me like I am nothing but a body. The reporters. They talk about what I allege happened to my body. They talk about my parts that only add up to my whole (my hole) and nothing more. Like I am not more than the sum of my parts. I am only legs plus vagina plus arms and head and breasts, which were underdeveloped at the time of abuse. They talk about how I allege that he touched my parts. They talk about how I allege that he forced me to touch his parts.

Suzanna takes me to a big glittering downtown building surrounded by glass and concrete and marble and when we go inside it's all muted and hushed and plush and I feel blank and cold and I wish I hadn't worn shorts and a tank top, because I'm covered in goose bumps.

They talk like I should have known better. The attorneys.

They ask why I didn't say anything for so long. They ask why I didn't tell my parents. They ask why I didn't tell a teacher. They ask why now. They ask do I remember when it started. Do I remember how old I was. Do I remember what grade I was in. Do I remember how often I played at his house with his daughter. They ask do I remember how often I was alone with him. They ask how much did you weigh at the time, do you remember? They ask how tall were you, do you remember? They ask if he showed me pornography before or after the first incident of abuse. They ask what type of pornography. They ask if I can describe it to them. They ask do I remember what he said. They ask do I remember what parts of his touched what parts of mine. They ask do I remember, do I remember, like I probably forgot and they want me to admit it. They ask why did I say in my statement that it started the winter I was eleven when I'm saying now it started that fall. They ask if I'm sure it was him, if I'm sure it wasn't so-and-so-who-was-friends-with-my-dad-at-the-time, if I'm sure it was me, if I'm sure it was in my bed and in his living room and in his bathroom and one time in the park when he was supposed to be walking me home. They ask me if I remember if he, that time, if he verbally suggested it or if he forced my parts onto his parts or if he didn't say anything at all and I just offered to. They ask if I ever verbally protested or expressed that I didn't consent like did I ever say I don't consent to this. They ask me if I'm sexually active. They ask me if I have a boyfriend. They ask me about the video online. They ask me if I remember what happened. They ask me if I've ever to my knowledge been raped, sexually assaulted, sexually harassed.

They ask me if I drink. They ask me how often I get drunk. They ask me how often I black out.

They say I can go. They say they'll call me if they need me. They say thanks. They say have a good rest of your day.

We pull up in front of Ro's house and Rumi is sitting on the tire swing in her front yard. He's looking down at his feet and swinging side to side like a pendulum.

I get out of the car and Rumi looks up at me with emotions all over his face, but I can't process them.

Suzanna stops outside the front door and Ro is at the downstairs window and I watch as Noah joins her. I don't know what my face looks like right now.

Like a corpse. I look like a corpse, I think.

They're worried about me, Ro and Suzanna and Noah.

Rumi gets off the swing. "Virginia?" he says.

I wave at them. Suzanna goes inside and Ro frowns at me, then gestures Noah away from the window.

"What?" I say to Rumi.

"Please, Virginia, can we talk?"

I almost laugh because it's just like what I said to him. When I tried to tell him. And when he didn't listen. I turn to go inside. I don't want to do this.

He puts his hand on my arm, gentle but insistent, and I whip around. "Don't touch me!" He snatches his hand away like I breathed fire in his face. I wrap my arms around myself and realize I'm shaking. "You can't just touch me! You can't just expect me to be okay around you, Rumi! You broke my fucking heart!"

"Okay, okay," he says. He presses his hands to his face. We're standing here on the sidewalk. A woman dodges around us, tugging a toddler along behind her. I watch them walk, little brown legs, little chubby feet wrapped in sandals, guided along. "Okay," Rumi says again. "I won't. I won't touch you. I know I fucked up. I know it can't be like it was between us." He's shaking too. "You were right," he says.

"I know."

"About Lyra," Rumi says.

"Yeah, Rumi, I know. This is the moment where you come and tell me how wrong you are and I, like, forgive you and say it's okay, but it's not okay and I'm not going to do that."

He stares at me like he wants me to absolve him. "It's my fault," he says. "I almost let it happen."

"How could you not believe me?" I say. "After everything?"

He pinches the skin between his eyes, the bridge of his nose, and wipes his tears away. He looks at me one last time and then walks away with his hands in his pockets.

"What did he want?" Ro asks as soon as I come into the house.

I shake my head and reach for her hand. "I don't know."

She gives me a look.

"He wanted me to tell him it's okay he fucked off and ignored me when I needed him."

"Hah," she says.

"Watch your language," Suzanna says to me.

"How many syllables is *dystopian*?" Noah says, staring at his phone.

Suzanna sets down her cup. "Dys-to-pi-an," she counts out, holding her fingers.

"Four, that's what I thought," he says.

"What are you doing?" Ro asks.

"Sending a haiku to my brother."

Suzanna gives him a quizzical look.

"We communicate in haikus now," Noah says.

"How long has that been going on?" Suzanna says.

"About a year?"

"Nerd," Ro says.

Up in Ro's room my face must look like something, because Ro pokes me in the cheek and says, "What?"

"It's just, Lyra. Me and then years go by and then Lyra. And I just happen to know her. What are the chances?"

Ro puts her phone down and looks at me.

"Like, you know. Statistically. What are the odds that I would just happen to know the one other person he targeted?"

She hesitates and I see something behind her mouth and eyes. "You? Did he? With you?" I say, wondering how come I'm not screaming.

"I think he tried. Almost." She sits back on her heels.

"But, when?"

"I like, I didn't even identify it as what it was until you told me about him. Then I remembered."

"What happened?"

Ro sticks her fingernail in her mouth, chewing on her neon shellac until I tug her hand away.

"Please tell me," I say.

"I don't want to burden you, though, because nothing actually happened especially compared to you."

"Don't do that. What happened to you matters too. I think, I think we need to talk about this. I think it might be a really big deal. How many? Honestly, Ro, how many of us?"

She looks like she wants to cry. "I don't know."

"Tell me what happened."

She nods and smooths the cotton of her pants over her thighs, then clasps her hands together in her lap, knuckles tight. "It was Thalia's birthday party. When we were, when she turned ten. Remember? My parents were gone for the weekend and I had to spend Saturday night too. They didn't want to let me. You know how Mom and Dad are."

I nod and she shrugs and keeps going. "But I so desperately wanted to go to this stupid sleepover. I would miss it unless I could stay both nights. I made a PowerPoint presentation about the importance of peer group bonding and rites of passage. I'd actually never been to a slumber party at that point."

"Right," I say, and I manage to smile a little.

"So they let me."

I wait.

"That Saturday after the party, Thalia fell asleep on the couch with her mom. I stayed up until the end of the movie. We were watching *Scream*. I was shocked that they let us. I mean, god, totally inappropriate for ten-year-olds, right?"

I shrug.

"When it was over they were both asleep, Thalia and her mom, stretched out on the couch. There wasn't any room for me and I can't sleep with the TV on anyway so I went to Thalia's room."

I'm quiet because I know what's coming.

"He came in and sat on the edge of the bed after I was in my pajamas and ready to sleep. It was late, like almost midnight. The light was off. He put his hand on my ankle and talked to me. I think he was testing me out. Thinking about it now."

"Yeah. He was."

"But I got up and I was like, *I need water! I'm hungry!* And he tried to tell me he would get me a snack but I got loud. I talked really loud and woke up Thalia's mom. She came and got me and told me to come watch this great movie and it was just the second half of some dumb seventies thing." Ro stops and looks at her hands for a minute. "So I slept the rest of the night wedged on the end of the couch with Thalia and her mom. I didn't actually sleep much. When my mom and dad came and got me the next day I didn't know what to say. It felt so creepy and weird, but nothing actually happened. Maybe I was just crazy. But I told them about sleeping on the couch and watching *Scream* and I think they got the idea that Thalia's parents weren't very structured. There's no bedtime and no screen time limits and they let us watch R-rated movies. So. They never let me spend the night again. When Thalia would ask I would just be like, *Aw my parents said no*. And that's it. That's the whole story."

"I don't know why I didn't think. I don't know why I thought I was special."

She shudders. "Don't say it like that."

We just sit in silence for I don't know how long, until she says, "I have to tell, don't I?"

And I'm not sure if my life is ending, or my life is beginning, or if this is just normal now, when Ro calls for her mom and dad and we get ready to tell them about how bad things actually are. There is a chill and a hush as they come like they know. Suzanna sits on the bed and Noah sits at Ro's desk and Ro and me hold hands and sit crisscross-applesauce on the floor like we're in preschool and I kind of wish we were.

Nobody says anything until Suzanna says, "It's okay, love, whatever you need to tell us, it's okay. We'll make it okay." It's only Suzanna fiddling with her delicate gold necklace, sliding the pendant back and forth, back and forth, that gives it away. How nervous she is.

I squeeze Ro's hand and she tells them.

Noah stands up suddenly and walks out of the room. Before any of us can react he's back and he pulls Ro to standing and wraps his strong brown arms around her and hugs her so tight, I start to cry. But I keep it quiet because I know this moment isn't about me. It's just that it breaks my heart in the strangest way to see a dad doing what he should in a moment like this. Not like my dad.

They're both crying about what almost happened and Suzanna sits there on Ro's bed looking shocked. They're still hugging when Suzanna starts to talk. She says, "So both of you, Virginia and Ramona. What about Thalia? What about Paz? What about Poppy?"

"How many of us?" I say.

Suzanna nods like I got the question right. "I need to call Paz's mom."

And so they leave us alone again and eventually Paz comes creeping up the stairs, while the grown-ups murmur in the kitchen. She puts her legs across my lap and leans her head on my neck and holds me tight. I feel her reach back for Ro and Ro wraps her arms around the two of us and for a while we just rock, bodies overlapping.

But then we have to talk. We sit in a circle, our knees touching, in the dim bedroom light. I feel a strange magic here, of the three of us in a circle, together, loving each other fiercely, whispering, telling our secrets, telling our stories. The inexplicable magic of saying the words out loud. Ramona tells Paz what happened to her and of course she already heard what happened to me.

"Did it happen to you too?" Ro asks Paz.

Paz pushes her hair out of her face, and her eyes look huge.

I wait. I don't know what she's going to say.

"*I don't know,*" Paz says.

Me and Ro look at each other quick, then back to Paz.

She keeps going. "Me and Thalia, we've been friends for so

long. And our parents, I mean my mom and her mom, they're both immigrants. They have, like, a bond or whatever. I've been spending nights over there since before I can even remember." She shivers and rubs her bare arms, up and down, up and down, then puts her hands back into ours and our circle is complete again. "There are a lot of things I don't remember," Paz says. "All those trips we took that everybody talks about? Like to Lake Chelan and Victoria? *I don't remember them*. I mean, maybe a few things like inner-tubing and Butchart Gardens. But most of it? Completely blank."

Paz tightens her grip on my hand and says, "I think I block trauma out. Like, I don't remember when Edison was calling me transphobic slurs in second grade. I blocked it out. What else have I blocked out?"

A muscle in my lip starts twitching and I bite down on it.

"And remember when I went through that phase of showing boys my underwear? I mean, I thought I was just excited about my Phineas and Ferb undies, but that's not normal, is it? It's actually a sign of abuse. Remember when I started wetting the bed? Around when I was eleven. That's a sign of abuse too."

"Oh Paz," I say, because I can't keep it in, because all these things are so familiar. The bed-wetting and the showing of private parts and the patchy memory.

"But I don't remember anything. I don't remember any actual, like, incidents. I do remember that at some point Thalia got super clingy. She wouldn't even let me go to the bathroom alone. I think it was when we were eleven because it started when we did swim camp and that was the summer before sixth grade. And we started spending most of the time at my house. I didn't really notice, but I think it was her. She would be like, *You have all the good channels, you have the comfy bed, your mom always lets us play video games.* I wonder if . . ." But she stops like she can't bear to finish.

"If she knew?" Ro says.

Paz nods.

"Maybe that's why she invited me that one year," I say. "To New Mexico, when we were eleven."

Paz clasps her hands to her mouth, horrified. "Oh my god, Virginia! Is that when it started? Is it my fault?"

"Stop. No. Of course not, Paz! Don't do that!"

Ramona grabs both of our hands again and takes a deep breath before saying, "We're not going to do that. It's his fault. All of it."

We stare at one another.

"What now?" I finally say.

We listen to the moms talking, a low soothing croon.

"Is that Willow?" Paz says, tilting her head.

"I wish Poppy were here," I say, but nobody answers.

They say there are others. The reporters. Then the attorneys. They say other victims have come forward.

. . .

They say he is considering a plea deal.

They say those other girls just want attention. They say those other girls just want a book deal. They say they just want their fifteen minutes. They say they just want to get followers. They say they just want to go on *Oprah*.

They say there is a new victim. They say her name. They say she wants to speak.

She's on the steps of some official-looking building. Willow is standing behind her. The ticker tape below her scrolls by: *Prominent community leader accused of multiple counts of child sexual abuse*, like it's not devastating and horrifying and validating all at the same time.

We're both watching and we're both crying. Ro's hand is gripping mine and I'm digging my fingers into the furrows of the carpet.

"It happened to me too," Poppy says, and I wish this image weren't quite so sharp and clear. "She isn't lying. He abused me as well." And she steps back and Willow leans into the microphone and starts talking about justice and truth and making the community safe again.

It's like wave after wave is hitting me and my skull is vibrating from the impact. It happened to her too. When? How many times? When did it stop? Was it like with me? Over and over and over? But how? For me it stopped when she moved here and I started spending nights at her house. She gave me somewhere to escape to. When he came over, I went to Poppy's house. She saved me from him.

How when how where how did it happen to her?

Who saved *her*?

What if nobody saved her?

I'm gripping my head. I can feel my skull through my skin through my hair I can feel my frontal bone and my temporal bone and my zygomatic bone pushing my fingers against it under my eyes until I feel like my eyeballs are going to explode from the pressure.

"Virginia?" Ramona is talking to me.

"How many of us?" I say to her as she peels my fingers off my skin and grips them.

Twenty-three

TIME IS LIKE the throb of a bruise. Each minute that passes by is a deep aching pulse. I pretend like it's not. I chat with Suzanna. I help Ro wash the dishes and then we look up hostels in France for her as-yet-hypothetical backpacking trip next summer. But the whole time I'm waiting and itching and then I can't help it anymore and I stand at the window and watch for nothing, for something, for I-don't-know-what.

(Poppy. I watch for Poppy. I watch her house.)

Poppy left. She left. She left me here. I come back to it again and again like the same throbbing bruise.

She left me here. She left me here.

But why?

Why did she disappear?

Thalia's dad abused her too.

I turn to Ro. "When Poppy left," I start, and then I stop. I think my face is blank. Staring at nothing.

"What?" Ro says.

"When Poppy left, it was when Thalia told me that some program director for soccer broke her whole body or something. Was it a car accident? I don't remember. And Thalia's dad had to step in as the program director. And Poppy was supposed to coach a team. Lyra's team. And then she left. That's when she left. That's when she disappeared. It was when Thalia's dad took over and he was going to be super involved in the soccer program for the whole summer."

Ro's face looks like mine feels. Shocked. "She left so she didn't have to be around him?"

"She *fled*, Ro. She bolted. She must have totally freaked out when she realized he was going to be there *all the time*."

"Holy shit," Ro says.

"And then he coached Lyra's team. Because Poppy left. And he had to step in to coach her team. That's how he met Lyra."

"Holy shit," Ro says again.

It echoes around me. The one, two, three, the simple things that led like dominoes to him taking over, Poppy leaving, him meeting Lyra, and then to me telling. Because Lyra was in danger. Because Poppy left. Because he took over. Because some random program director got into a car accident.

According to court records, he said, "She was a willing participant."

A willing participant.

The worst part of admitting that something wrong happened to me are the feelings that sweep me along in their wake, the feelings that I am not sure I can ever keep my head above, the feelings that will possibly probably drown me, the feelings that I'm afraid are too much too great too terrible too horrible too terribly sad to ever overcome.

. . .

Ro says let's go for a run, let's go to the grocery store, let's go swimming, let's go do something, anything, it doesn't matter, just let's go be in public.

She's sitting at her desk, using clear nail polish to decoupage a jewelry box. She picks up a clipping from a magazine, some unrecognizable photo cut into the shape of a feather or a flame, and paints it onto the box.

I'm here all the time now. My mom, Suzanna said, couldn't seem to face it. My abuse. My mom was sure it must be a misunderstanding. She was sure I was just confused. She was sure. Suzanna couldn't even get my dad on the phone.

Ro says I can stay here. Or maybe I could get a job and an apartment. I'm almost eighteen. I could get my GED. Move to another city. Olympia or Portland or Santa Clara. I could change my name. Cut my hair, dye it pink. Nobody will know me. I won't be That Girl. My identity will be more than the people I've fucked. More than the things that have happened to me.

"Let's wash our faces, brush our teeth, and drink some coffee. Just to start," Ro says, still trying to convince me to go somewhere.

We walk through the foot traffic of The Ave to a playground down the street where Ro says Langston and Paz are waiting. Eyes graze my skin like fingers. No, my name didn't get out, but somehow it's like everybody knows anyway. Maybe they don't. Maybe I'm imagining it. Or maybe they are all looking. Maybe they were always looking.

And men. They leer. They leer in that possessive intrusive arrogant unabashed way they have of leering.

Paz runs to us. She draws us into her arms and hugs us tight and hums into my hair and we hug until Langston takes my hand and kisses my cheek and smiles at me.

It's almost normal, being here. We sit on a blanket in the grass and watch a group of middle schoolers scuffle on the basketball court. Isaiah and some other kids are playing hacky sack and Edison is rolling around on a skateboard. Langston lies on the blanket next to Paz. Paz puts her feet on my lap and for a minute all is well.

Edison glances at me and smirks. He angles his skateboard and cuts it close to my feet, so close that I yank them back onto the blanket. Ro leans forward and Paz puts her feet under her butt like she's ready to jump up. Their faces are identical masks. Edison wheels by again, close and grating, and gravel flies in my face.

I shrink back at the same time as the others leap up.

"Fuck off!" Ro throws her empty water bottle at Edison. Langston pulls himself up and steps in front of Paz.

The next time Edison comes by, Langston pushes him off the skateboard. "Seriously. Stop. You're being a dick."

Ro yanks me up and into her side, her arm wrapped tight around me.

Edison rolls his eyes.

"After everything she's been through—" Langston says.

"She *says* she's been through," Edison cuts him off.

Like, *allegedly*.

Like, I'm just some bitch smearing a good man's name.

All the words fill my head. The violent words. The sexual assault words. The rape words. All the words of the people who think I'm lying.

Edison stands there, smug like he owns the world and nobody can touch his white-upper-middle-class-straight-cis-boy self, and for a second I see red like literally my vision becomes tinged with red because he's right.

Nobody can touch him. He'll be fine, no matter what. No matter what a shitty shitty asshole he is. He'll go to a good college, get a good job, marry some poor beautiful woman who is way too good for him and treat her like crap and still she won't leave him and he'll be fine. Because nobody can touch him through the force field that is his privilege.

Except me. I can touch him.

And then I'm striding forward and I shove him and he stumbles back and starts to mouth off to me but I don't hear him because I'm picking up his skateboard and swinging it at his face and then there is a smack and a crunch and he's flat on his back with shock all over his face and blood flowing from his nose into his mouth into his ears.

Then he jumps up and I'm still too filled with rage to feel afraid in the brief second that he pulls his fist back and then he drives it into my mouth and the pain that fills my skull is like an electric shock. It spreads from my skin to my teeth to my jaw to my ears to my throat. I rock back on my heels and almost fall before I catch myself. My mouth fills with blood.

Paz and Langston and Ro and Isaiah and all the other people standing around laughing talking bullshitting who were stunned and frozen, they start moving. Isaiah grabs Edison and hauls him back. Paz tries to touch my face but I swat her hand away and lunge for Edison. Langston locks his arms around me and I can't move and Edison laughs at me.

"Cunt," he says. "Fucking psycho," he says.

I spit a mouthful of blood right in his fucking face.

"Fuck you!" I snarl at him. "Fuck you, Edison! Fuck you fuck you fuck you fuck you," I shout at him like I *am* a fucking psycho and I want to rip his face off like Hannibal Lecter. Langston is dragging me away and Ro is running next to me and I look back and Paz is shouting something at Edison and Isaiah is shaking his head like he's shocked and Edison is wiping blood off his face and laughing.

I wake up with a headache. My temples pound and my jaw throbs and even my skin hurts. The bruise isn't so bad. It makes me wonder if I'm a weenie. It just looks like I'm extra tired, with dark purple circles under my eyes. And a grayish blue splotch on the left side of my jaw. I don't have the makeup to cover it and it probably wouldn't really work anyway.

Paz watches me examining my bruise. She breaks into an unwilling smile, showing her teeth just a little, then smothers it with her hand. "I'm really glad you hit him with the skateboard," she says.

I stayed with Paz last night. I braid her silky powdered-sugar-smelling hair and she leans her head against my shoulder. "Langston told his parents about Williams. I guess it's really happening."

"Were they mad?" I ask.

She shrugs. "Not really. He's, like, so passionate about it. Wanting to be a children's librarian. And it's such a sweet ambition. It's hard to be mad. I love him so much."

I tie off her braid and put my chin on her shoulder and at the same time as I feel so happy for her, I also feel such deep sadness and I miss Rumi so much. "You're so lucky, Paz," I say, and I think she can tell what I'm feeling.

She twists around and puts her arms around me. "Do you still love him?"

I nod into her neck. "I wish I didn't."

She pulls away and puts her hands on my cheeks. "Poor Virginia. I bet you wish you could just get the fuck out of here."

"Oh my god, so much," I say.

Twenty-four

I JUST STOPPED going to tutoring. I'm sure I'm not the first person to stop showing up, but I still feel guilty. I still feel like I have to hide. Not just from tutoring, but from everybody.

I keep thinking about Lyra and her quick small body. I keep thinking about the strangeness of my own body that I've felt. All these years like it's not really mine and I don't want it anyway. I keep thinking about how she loves to play soccer and about how Thalia's dad was her coach. I think about the way I run. At first it was penance, like my guilt ran down my skin with sweat, and then later like my sweat was a tithe to my strong body, to my strong soul. Like my body, maybe it is mine after all. Maybe I do want it.

I text her first and ask permission. Tell her to ask Aunt Jennifer.

YES!!! comes back.

did you ask your aunt?

YESSSSSSSS

what did she say?

SHE SAID YAAAASSSSSS hurry up when are you coming

right now git yer running shoes

"Lyra!" I call when I'm outside.

She comes bounding out the door and runs down the front steps so fast, I think she might fall but she doesn't.

"Do you want to talk?" I say. Now that it's out and she probably knows.

"About what?"

I sit down on the stairs. "About, you know, him. Kermit the Frog."

Lyra flushes, deep crimson staining her cheeks. Is she angry? Embarrassed? Does she know how close he got? Did she ever feel it? Like a shiver down her spine?

"You should have told *me*," she says. "Not Rumi."

"But you're—" I start.

She raises an eyebrow. "Just a kid?"

It's like she punched me in the gut. The hypocrisy of my impulse to tell Rumi, not her. To not even try to tell her what could have happened *to her*. What happened to me when I was *her age*.

When I can breathe I stand up and hold my arms out to her. She buries her head in my chest, her arms around my waist, and I hold her tight. It's like she's been waiting for it. Waiting to be hugged. Encompassed. Loved. Safe.

"I'm sorry," I say. "I'm sorry about everything. I'm sorry this happened. I'm sorry I didn't tell you first. I should have."

She pulls away. "It's okay. Just . . . be my friend. Okay?" Love her fiercely. That's what she's asking.

"Okay. I will," I promise. I will. I promise myself too. I will. "Are you ready to run?"

"Yes!" she shouts to the sky.

"Do you have your phone? I'm sharing a playlist with you."

Lyra smiles at me, haloed by her giant blue headphones, dark baby hairs curling around her face.

"Let's sync up," I say, and mouth *one two three*, and it comes on. Kinetic beats and lyrics that tweak my brain and lyrics that make me feel proud of my existence in this body in this world and lyrics that make me want to dance.

Lyra high-steps, her feet landing on the beat. I catch up to her and shake my shoulders and shimmy and put my hands up in the air and she does a move like a sprinkler and I do a lawn mower. She laughs with her eyes closed but I can't hear her and then we start running.

The sun shines on us and there is a little wind and I can smell the peaches dripping juice. We run and then we run faster and then faster until we're both sprinting as hard as we can. She's almost faster than me and there is joy in all the lines of her body and I feel like crying but I don't. I whoop and I can't hear myself. Lyra sees my whoop and I think she screams, but I can't hear her.

We fall into a stride. Her joy, my joy, burns down into pride. Proud of these bodies. Proud of what they can do. Proud of ourselves for running even though we're breathing hard and sweating. Proud of our power.

Where is Thalia? She's disappeared just like Poppy. I don't think she's actually gone, though. I think she's just hiding in her house. I can see her windows from Ro's. They're covered, always covered. All of them. The bottom windows, under the eaves, they're thick peach velvet. Thalia's dad hung them up sometime around when I was eleven. I remember them going up. I remember feeling trapped within them.

In Thalia's room are white curtains. They are thin and diaphanous with lace edges. They used to remind me of Anne of Green Gables in a summer dress floating in a wooden riverboat.

I remember sitting with Thalia and her dad at the wrought iron table in the backyard surrounded by summer blooms and drifting bees and butterflies floating by like fairies. I remember the colorful pictures of goddesses riding chariots spread out before us. I remember how both me and Thalia were fascinated by their power. I remember how at a certain age Thalia disavowed our favorite princesses, Tiana and Belle and Ariel, claiming they were for little kids. I remember how we would argue about fairy tales versus mythology versus folktales. How I thought it was all basically the same and how she disagreed.

It occurs to me now that Thalia had a point. Fairy tales have a lot of princesses or maybe just women in distress. Princesses and witches. Women have very specific defined roles.

Mythology, there's usually some goddesses hanging around. A goddess, she can be a lot of different things. She contains multitudes. She can even shape-shift if she feels like it. She can be wrathful, she can be benign, she can be generous, she can be vengeful, she can be conniving, she can be benevolent. A goddess is complicated. It's in her nature. She can't be defined by any one role. She's a witch, a princess, a friend, but she's also powerful.

One thing a goddess has that a tower-trapped princess doesn't have? Power.

I watch a dark shape move around behind Thalia's white curtains. Just a princess hiding in her tower. Afraid to leave. A princess who has no power. Or a princess who *thinks* she has no power.

Thalia's dad, I hate saying his name. I can't say it or maybe I won't. I think it's that I won't. To me, he has no name. I take his name away. He is a nameless monster, a beast. And the beast, the wolf, the monster, he gave me a gift. The power to tell my story. The belief and knowledge that telling my story gives me power. And now I am using it to make sense of what he did to me. He gave me the tools to defeat him. Isn't that somewhere in the hero's journey? Isn't that classic mythology? Or is it fairy tales?

I don't have much money saved, but I like the idea of buying something new. Something that is small and beautiful and mine. Something to mark this new life, this new, this more real version of me.

I wander the aisles of the farmer's market, touching prisms and plants and the ridges of oil paintings. I'm examining a ceramic mug when Thalia approaches me. I haven't seen her since . . . Since.

"Hey." She's clutching a lumpy paper bag in front of her chest like a shield.

I feel a pain that starts in my heart and swoops into my gut and takes my breath away.

"Can we talk?" she says.

I scan the crowd behind her, to the left, to the right. There's no protection order, there's nothing to stop him, there's nobody here with me.

"He's not here," Thalia says.

My hands are shaking. I tighten them around the cup. There's a crack in the ceramic filled with blue resin. Thalia is watching me with narrowed eyes. She seems annoyed by my anxiety, but then her cheeks flush and her eyes fill with tears but they don't fall.

"Are you going to buy that?" She points to the mug.

It's lovely and for a moment I consider it. But I put it back ever so carefully because I know that every time I touch it I will remember this moment. The fear of facing her dad. The way my fingers trembled against the ceramic.

We sit under a frothing honeysuckle vine. The fragrance of the blossoms distracts me for a moment. I don't know what to expect.

"I had an abortion," Thalia says.

"What?"

"About a month ago." Her eyes somehow look too big for her skull. "I felt like I was going crazy. There was no way I was going to keep it. I didn't expect Edison to want to like *raise a baby* with me, but he was such a dick about it. I thought at least he could be supportive of the process. He was like, *how do I know it's mine?*"

I shake my head.

"So fucking cliché," Thalia says. "I ended up going to the clinic with Paz before everything . . . you know."

The quick hard crash of my heart won't slow.

"I hate this. I hate all of it." She sweeps her hand over her thin tan legs, flat belly, round breasts. Like her body has betrayed her. Like it hasn't done the things it was supposed to do. "How can I ever get past this? Any of it. I feel like, I feel like . . ." she says, struggling for words.

"Like the devastation left after a catastrophe," I say.

"Like a smoking radioactive crater."

Empty and aching.

"I'm sorry." My throat hurts.

"For what?"

"For Edison." That's what I meant. But I wonder what else I should apologize for. It's a strange thing facing the daughter of my abuser now that it's out and she knows.

"It's not your fault." She glances sideways at me. "Well, some of it is."

I nod but then I stop because it's not my fault. Not any of it, I don't think. "Wait," I say, because I think she's going to keep talking. "The thing is, the first time it happened with Edison it wasn't, like, consensual," I say, repeating Rumi's words. "I said no to him. Over and over and over and he just kept on."

Thalia is nodding. She's looking down at her knees. I watch

as she wipes at her eyes with a finger, careful of her mascara and eyeliner. "Yeah," she says, like it sounds familiar.

I say, "And that's what it was like. It was always like he just kept pushing me and pressuring me until I had to say yes and act like I liked it or else it was like I was admitting to myself that what was happening wasn't consensual, and if it wasn't consensual, then, like, what was it? It was sexual assault. And I just . . . I'm so sick of this happening to me. Over and over. It's easier to like it. To pretend like I choose it and I like it. But I didn't and I don't and—" I stop and look at Thalia again.

Tears are running down her face. Her eyes are rimmed with black that's spreading a little and it's beautiful. She looks like a photograph.

"And people treated me like I was some slut for it. For being assaulted by Edison over and over. People acted like it was my fault. Even though they all know what he's like. *You* know what he's like and you blamed me for it anyway."

"I know," she says. "You're right."

"But I'm not a slut. I don't even know if a slut is, like, a real thing. People are just trying to figure themselves out, right? What even is a slut? It's not even anything. And even in those moments when I did consent to things with Edison, even those moments I don't feel clear about. Like, what does consent look like in an abusive relationship? Is it even possible to consent in an abusive relationship?"

"And Edison *is* abusive," Thalia says. She wipes at more tears. "God," she says, "am I ever going to stop crying?"

I sigh and shake my head and say, "Right? Probably not."

"It was like that with me too. I was just stupid enough to think I was in love with him." Her smile is flat on her face like somebody slapped it on. It's not a real smile, but it's not meant to be.

"I've been going to this therapist," she says. "She's the one who told me to apologize to you. I didn't want to. She said it's part of my recovery process."

"Apologize to me?"

"For that night. For the night of the party when you passed out, and . . ."

And.

"And we. Me and Edison. And we wrote on you and . . . my therapist, she kept going on about revictimization and how it's really common for survivors of sexual abuse."

(It's her dad that abused me.)

"To have substance abuse problems and unhealthy sexual relationships. She also said that what happened that night was assault." She starts to cry again. It's different this time. It is sudden and intense. I frown at my feet until she wipes at the mascara under her eyes and sighs.

"I am really sorry, Virginia. It was a really fucked up thing to do to you. I'll never forgive myself."

"I don't even really remember. All I know is what I saw on that video."

She shudders a little. "That wasn't me who put it out there."

"I know."

"Do you want to know what happened?"

Do I?

She goes on anyway like she is in a confessional. "We drew on your legs. I guess you probably saw that. All the way up to your underwear. They wanted, Edison and those guys, they wanted me and Liz to, like, go under it and draw, you know, but we didn't."

I don't say anything.

"Edison and them kept egging us on, telling us to do more. It started out kind of funny, but then it felt really creepy and wrong. Even if Ro hadn't come in I wouldn't have done anything else."

"But you were yelling at her, I remember."

"Yeah, when she came in. I was so drunk. And so angry. At you, at Edison, at myself for staying with him all those months even though I knew what he was doing."

There are birds on the honeysuckle. We sit so still, Thalia and I, that they rustle and hop from branch to branch, and the butterflies float and flutter and land, and I wonder and I wonder and I wonder, where do we go from here?

There is one thing left unsaid. And I don't know how to say it.

There is so much I don't know. There is so much I never thought about, because I was so busy un-thinking all the things I couldn't cope with.

How do you grow up in a house with a sexual predator? How do you live with a pedophile? How do you exist every day with a dad who is sexually attracted to little girls?

Especially when you are a little girl.

Thalia and I are so much alike. Our appeal is not enigmatic. It's not complex or compelling. It's easy. It's accessible.

We are the same.

We are victims.

Of the same people.

We are victims of the same people.

I must look different than I did a moment ago, because Thalia's face closes off. She leans back and narrows her eyes and crosses her arms.

"I don't want to talk about my dad," she says.

"But did you—" I start.

"I don't want to talk about him."

"But did he, I mean . . ." I try again.

"I don't want to talk about it!"

I stop because I know what it's like to have a secret so awful that you can't face the telling of it.

"I have to leave anyway," Thalia says.

"Please don't go."

"I have to meet my therapist." But she doesn't stand up.

It's like my lines are blurred. They're bleeding into her lines. We overlap and I see that now. I wish I had been able to see it before.

Twenty-five

I FEEL THIS kind of itchy restlessness. I check my phone, scroll, scroll, put it down, pick it back up.

I am tired of this. This living in my fingertips.

I want to exist in the dripping eaves. The wind I can hear instead of feel because it is too high in the trees. The way my red toenails look against the moss-colored, chevron-patterned blanket. I want this whole body. This whole life.

I want to love my life.

Every day of it.

I don't want to cringe and skulk and hide. Or otherwise be outrageous and brash and promiscuous as if I have to own this identity that I've found myself in, this self-perpetuating, self-loathing, self-fulfilling prophecy of a life I've been living. All because I'm afraid of being caught. As if existing in this molested skin is a crime I'm somehow guilty of.

I want to love my body. I want to bare skin or cover skin based on nothing more than the pleasure of how I look and feel under however much silk or cotton or linen I'm wearing. I want to show my body to people who I choose to see it and not show it to people who I don't choose to see it.

I want to kiss somebody I'm attracted to. I want to linger in that kiss. I want to wander deeper into that kiss and whatever lies beyond it.

I want to have good sex. I want to love it and do it again and again and again and again and again, and then I want to stop when I feel like stopping.

I want to love my existence in this world.

I want to love myself.

I see Rumi through the sun-smudged window. I feel the heat and light on my face and for a moment I don't know how I will react to him.

I knew this would happen.

He knocks and I pull the door open. I know there is expectation on my face.

He reaches out and trails his fingers along my arm, over the bumping bone of my wrist, and takes my hand.

I feel breathless.

"I'm sorry," he says.

The sun is behind his head, and the primroses and the hyssop and the hellebores are fragrant and heady in the heat and this feels surreal and I think he might kiss me and then he does.

The taste of his mouth, and the scent of him, and the feel of his skin under the sliding fabric of his shirt, and the way he presses the whole of his body along the whole of mine.

It doesn't happen like that.

He knocks but I don't answer. I can't face him. Or maybe I won't. I could but I choose not to. He is the one who ended our friendship. And I have no interest in this thrown bone. I walk away from his stunned face on the other side of the window and my reflected image in the glass and I walk into the backyard and lie in the sun and close my eyes and soak up the heat and eventually I stop thinking about him and I never think about him again.

It doesn't happen like that either.

His skin beneath his white shirt is tan and smooth. I miss the feel of it, but then, I never really had the right to touch him. The facets of his face, his body, the way he moves. As he comes to the door each detail is significant in its indifference. It's just the way he exists, but it makes me ache.

He knocks and I answer but I step outside instead of letting him in.

I feel thin and bruised.

"I really do love you, Virginia." He says *Virginia* like a caress. Like he loves me. Like my identity is safe in his mouth.

And in response love wells up behind my eyes and falls down as tears and I love him back but I don't say it and I won't. Not today. "I'm angry at you," I say. Say the words.

"I know," he says. "You should be. When you told about him, about Thalia's dad, and I realized that you were right about him and Lyra and when I realized that I didn't listen, it was like an awakening for me. And I wanted to explain something to you because I think you deserve to hear it. Why, maybe, I couldn't accept that you noticed something that I didn't. If you want to hear it, I want to tell you."

I feel something on my arm and look down. There is a ladybug on my wrist. As soon as I notice it, it flies away, dodging around Rumi as it goes. "Okay," I say.

"Do you want to sit?" He points to his car.

I lean back against the headrest and close my eyes.

"When my mom died . . . My mom died, remember?"

"Yeah," I say, and my voice is soft.

"I feel like it's my fault."

"But she had a stroke, right? How could that be your fault?"

"She was an alcoholic. I barely saw her because she was always passed out by the time I got home from school. Lyra was so little. And the house was disgusting and she puked all the time and she smelled awful. She just . . . She wasn't there. Me and Lyra went to live with my aunt."

He leans forward and presses his head into the steering wheel. "I hadn't talked to her for about a year before she died. She called me all the time. She would call me five times in a row while I was at school. I knew she was drunk. When she died I felt so much guilt for ignoring her. And there's nothing I can do with it. Nothing I can do with the guilt. I'm just stuck with it. Now that she's dead."

"But it's not your fault," I say. I watch his jaw muscles ripple under his skin. He's so beautiful even now, even angry and tense and sad.

"I feel like it is my fault, though. I ignored her. Maybe if I had paid more attention, I would have realized how bad it was.

I should have realized. I should have told my aunt how bad it was. Maybe she could have gotten help. Gone to rehab. Or something. Anything. I should have done something. Instead I did nothing. Because I didn't fucking pay attention."

"That still doesn't sound like your fault, Rumi."

"There's more though," he says.

"Tell me the story," I say. "Just say the words."

"Once upon a time," Rumi says, and smiles. My smile is small in response. "Once upon a time when I was fifteen I got a craving to play my old Wii. I wanted to play golf. I waited until I knew my mom wouldn't be there. She always worked evenings at the corner store. I took the bus. I remember there was somebody smoking pot on the bus. They were in the back and I was sitting in the middle but I could still smell it. I didn't smoke very much at that point, so I really noticed. It was almost dark. It was that time of year when you can tell summer is coming because all of a sudden it's after dinner and you're thinking about going to bed and it's still light out and it makes you feel more awake, more alive. I had my earbuds in and I was listening to Eminem. It was my Eminem phase."

"We all had one," I say.

He keeps talking. "When I walked into our apartment I could smell it. All the familiar smells. The musty smell of a closed-up space. The sour smell of puke. The rotten apple juice smell of the alcohol in her sweat. It made me mad. As soon as I walked in I was mad. I didn't take my earbuds out. I assumed she wasn't there. It was all dark. I turned on all the lights and it was like she had just left everything exactly the way it was when we moved out. The bare mattresses, the old toys, the mess. But I couldn't find the Wii. So I checked her room.

"She was facedown on her bed. She wasn't even under the covers. Her nails were painted, I noticed that. Bright shiny red. She always painted her nails so nice. When I was little she would paint mine too. My dad hated it, but she didn't care."

Rumi stops talking. It's sudden. He presses his hands to his face. Covers his eyes. His shoulders shake. He's crying.

"Rumi," I say, and I feel like my heart is breaking for him. I put my arms around him, enclosing him, encompassing him, his whole self.

He pulls away. "I thought she was passed out. I thought she was drunk. I just left her. I left her. I left her." He says it again and again, crying, until I pull him back in, hold him tight, letting him cry into me, absorbing his tears.

"They said she probably died sometime that night. She had a stroke. She was just lying there dying and I left. I took my Wii and I fucking left."

I'm crying too now. I can't help it.

"She was there for three days before anybody found her."

"It's not your fault, Rumi. It's not! You were a kid. You *are* a kid. You're not supposed to parent your mom. It's her job to take care of you, not the other way around."

He just shakes his head.

"Rumi, it's okay to leave. When your parents treat you badly, when they don't take care of you, when they neglect you. It's okay to leave." I'm saying it to myself too. I can see my house from here. Vacant. Void. Unoccupied.

It's okay to leave. It's okay to leave. It's okay to leave.

I pull the mirror down and wipe my eyes, my smeared makeup. Something falls in my lap. It's a picture, folded in half. I can see an edge of blue sky. I feel Rumi looking at me as I unfold it. It's me at Cannon Beach. Smiling into the sky. It's me, in pursuit of awe. Me, happy. It hits me, past my bones, deeper than my heart, right in my soul. This picture of me as my truest, happiest self. He cherishes it.

I turn to Rumi and he's looking at me and right now I love him so much it hurts, but I can't. Even though I can see the hope on his face. I can't.

"I have to go," I say through the tears that are still flowing.

"Okay," he says. "Okay. Do you think we can . . ." But he doesn't finish.

We can what? I want to ask. But I don't.

So I answer it all. All of the unspoken things. "I don't know," I say. "Not today."

And then I say the next thing. The thing that is secret and hopeful and that brings me pain in the hoping of it. "Maybe someday." Maybe someday we can.

*L*isten now. Let me tell you a story. The story of Medea, the goddess, the witch, the woman. There is a little bit left to tell.

Once upon a time Jason swore an oath to the gods to love Medea forever. Jason broke that oath. Medea was a goddess. She had the power of the gods. They whispered her name. They let her reap her vengeance on Jason and Corinth.

I see her now. She looks a little something like this: tall, thick black curling hair. Strong, she is strong. Power radiates from her terra-cotta skin. She stands above her grief. It doesn't go away. It's still there. It will always be there, but she stands above it.

She summons the gods and they come. Helios, her grandfather, he comes in his chariot of the sun. Blazing so bright and hot, the people of Corinth, Jason, they look away. They can't behold Medea with their human eyes anymore.

She steps into the chariot carrying the bodies of her beloved beautiful children and she ascends. She rises. This is her apotheosis. They never tell this part of the story. The apotheosis of Medea.

She tells it now to me. She says, I rise.

So I'm telling it now to you. I'm telling this story. Medea took her power back. That's how the story really ends.

Twenty-six

SINCE ME AND Thalia talked at the farmer's market, we've been together, the four of us, almost all the time. Paz's house or Ro's. Not Thalia's. Even though Thalia's dad isn't there. Still. Not Thalia's or mine. We're just missing Poppy. I can't get used to this ache.

When Poppy didn't come home after the press conference I asked Willow where she was, where her grandpa lives. It was like she was waiting for it. Like she wants me to go get Poppy, to bring her home. It burns knowing how close Poppy was this whole time. Just across the sound.

I'm driving. I started this reckoning. Ro is sitting shotgun, of course. Paz and Thalia are in the back, holding hands, loving each other fiercely. We're all loving one another fiercely.

We're road-tripping it out to the coast. Through green blurs of old-growth forest and fields of gold-ripened grass and dying flowers. Ro hangs her arm out the window, riding the sycamore wind. Thalia falls asleep with her head on Paz's shoulder and Paz doesn't let go of Thalia's hand even after.

It's night when we get there. It's a ghost moon, an-almost-not-there moon, a remember-when-I-was-full-and-luscious? moon. Her grandpa knows we're coming. He knows and he left because he knows this is just an us thing. A just us five thing.

Me, Thalia, Ro, Paz. We've come for Poppy.

I hesitate, out of the car, standing on nervous feet, and Ro slips her hand into mine, Paz on my other side with Thalia clinging to her. We approach the house in a red-rover chain, holding tight.

Poppy appears in the window, rippling behind the glass. "No," she says, but we can't hear it.

She comes out onto the porch in her bare feet with tangled hair and big empty eyes. "No," she says again. "You can't be here. You all have to go."

The wind picks up and rushes along my skin into my hair and I get goose bumps and Ro tightens her hand in mine, feeling it too, the rightness of it, the magic here, now that we're all together.

"We're not leaving," I say.

She starts to back up. "I'm sorry, I am, but I can't I just can't deal with this I can't do it."

"Poppy," I say, "it's okay. It's all okay."

"It's not!" she screams at me, her skin turning red and her face stretching. "Just go!"

I falter, then continue forward. "We're not leaving."

"I just want to be alone!"

"What's the point of feeling all these things just, like, by yourself? Just let us be here for you, Poppy."

"I'm not okay," she says, and sits on the steps and puts her head in her hands.

We break the chain and surround her, sitting on the steps with her, enfolding her. She sobs into my neck and I hold her

and I cry too and Paz is shaking and Thalia presses her forehead into Poppy's shoulder, making wet circles on her shirt,
and Ro holds me while I hold Poppy.

"I'm not okay," Poppy says again and again.

"None of us is okay," I say.

We cry ourselves dry, all together, all of us.

Once upon a time there were five friends. That is the most of
what they were. They were friends. They loved one another
fiercely.

But then something bad happened. They stopped trust-
ing each other. They didn't know why exactly. They just, one
day, didn't want to tell each other their secrets anymore. They
stopped telling each other their stories.

And the five friends became something else. They were suddenly just five girls, alone.

But one of them, she decided she had to be brave. Be brave
and be the first one to tell her story. Be brave and be the first
one to tell her secret. To say the words: *Once upon a time there
was a beast, a wolf, a monster, who was also a man.*

Because there is magic in telling your story.

It turned out, it happened to be, that her friends had the
same secret, the same story hidden inside them.

And so they sat down in a circle, their knees touching, their
fingers entwining, to tell their stories. To say the words out
loud.

. . .

We gather dried mango and chocolate-covered cherries and hot Earl Grey in a thermos and sliced sharp cheddar and thick hearty bread. We pack blankets and pillows into bags and backpacks. We bring candles and matches and sticks of incense.

In the whispering forest we trail after Poppy. She leads us to a red cedar that is so big, the other trees give it space; so big, I can't see the top of it. It disappears into the night, gray and gray and gray.

We sit on blankets, our knees touching, our fingers threading, flickering flames and smoke in the middle of our circle.

"Let's run away," I say.

"We could buy an old school bus," Thalia says.

"We could strip its walls and replace it with white oak paneling," Paz says.

"And string lights," I say.

"And build bunk beds," Poppy says.

"But with Egyptian cotton sheets and Pendleton blankets," Ro says.

"Or we could buy a cabin," I say.

"In the mountains!" Ro says.

"And plant pumpkins and sweet peas and mint," Thalia says.

"And chop wood and have a fire every night," Paz says.

"And brew potions and stews in a big-bellied cauldron," Poppy says.

The wind rushes through our circle, tossing sparks and leaves and we smile, our wild hair around our wild eyes. The night approves. The wind is our messenger.

We plan our escape. It doesn't matter if it's real or not.

Someday it will be hard to remember this feeling.

Someday what I'm feeling in this moment will seem wistful and nostalgic.

But right now it's real.

Right now,

it's so real.

And they lived happily ever after.

I'm the one telling the story, after all.

Author's Note

Sitting down to write this, suddenly I'm crying. It has happened a lot, when I think about my story, and how grateful I am that I get to tell it. Virginia's story is not my story, but it's a lot like it.

Once upon a time, in preschool, I showed some boys my underwear. We were hiding under the play structure, up the hill from the classrooms. I remember that I didn't want to. I remember that I did it anyway. My teacher told my mom and my mom took me to a therapist. Because this wasn't the first thing that happened that made her worry that I had been molested.

I remember sitting on the floor of the therapist's office playing with one of those red rubber playground balls. The redness of it. The texture of it. I told my story and then a lot of bad things happened. My dad didn't believe me because it was his friend that I accused. My dad, I guess, thought it was all a big misunderstanding and we should sort it out. So my dad invited his friend over for dinner. Me and my sister were at our friend's house and my dad called us home. I remember his friend's wife sitting at the dinner table. I remember asking her if her husband, my dad's friend, my abuser, was there. I remember her smile. How strange it felt to see her smiling at me. I remember when she said yes, he was here, he was just in the bathroom. I remember the sound of the toilet flushing and the door opening. I don't remember anything after that.

My mom was not like Virginia's mom. She took my dad to court. We got a restraining order against my abuser. She kept me safe. There were good people in my life, like in Virginia's life, who fought to protect me.

For so many years I felt ashamed of my story. I still feel ashamed, like Virginia, like so many victims of abuse. I feel ashamed of the abuse. I feel ashamed of the trouble it caused, before and after I told my story. I feel ashamed that I alienated my dad and my dad's side of the family. It feels as if *they* forgave *me*, instead of the other way around. For years I worried that I had made up the abuse.

For years I acted on my trauma and shame. One story not many people tell is that revictimization is possible. My body was sexualized at a young age, so to this day I still sometimes feel as if my body is just for sex. I was abused again as a teenager. I was raped repeatedly as an adult. My concept of consent was so distorted that I didn't even realize it was rape until somebody pointed out to me that if I said no and then sex happened anyway, that was rape. You might remember that Virginia had a similar moment in this novel.

Trauma is a strange thing. It's like grief. It never goes away. It just evolves. You just adapt. This story ends when the characters' stories are still ongoing. We see Virginia begin to deal with her abuse but we don't see Paz's or Poppy's healing process, and we don't even see Thalia admit that she has been abused.

I believe that even though they all have a lot of work and tears and pain ahead of them, each of the five friends who were impacted by the abuse will be okay.

But not everybody who is abused is okay. There is a moment in *Ever Since* when Virginia implies she's considering suicide. We see her at the park, alone, taking her mom's pills, and considering drinking several bottles of liquor. According to a study conducted by the National Library of Medicine, "approximately 80 percent of those who attempted suicide had a history of child abuse. Poor mental health, financial difficulties, poor coping skills, and reporting a suicide plan were also associated with an increased prevalence of attempting suicide."[1]

When I was fifteen I attempted suicide. I sat on the floor of my kitchen and took pain killers while my mom and sister walked around me, talking and making dinner. They didn't notice. I knew at the time I was doing it because I wanted attention. Sometimes people say that like it's a bad thing, *wanting attention*. But I'm here to tell you, of course you deserve attention. I wanted my mom to see the pain I was going through. I wanted help. Even though she didn't notice at the time, I told my sister about my attempt. Together we told my mom. I got the help I needed and things got better, but it took a long time.

Virginia had very little support. She was painfully isolated. She became more isolated as she lost her connection with Poppy and then Rumi. She felt she had alienated all of her friends. I'm so glad she left the park, kept looking for

1 Martin MS, Dykxhoorn J, Afifi TO, Colman I. "Child abuse and the prevalence of suicide attempts among those reporting suicide ideation." *Soc Psychiatry Psychiatr Epidemiol.* 2016 Nov;51(11):1477-1484. doi: 10.1007/s00127-016-1250-3. Epub 2016 Jun 11. PMID: 27290608; PMCID: PMC5101274.

connection, kept trying to tell her story. I'm so glad she didn't give up. Sometimes it feels like nothing will ever be okay again, but it does get better. It got better for Virginia, it got better for me, and it will get better for you too.

I started writing *Ever Since* years and years ago. Virginia's story is the story of my heart, of my pain. For so long I've wanted to tell this story. The story of a girl who is in pain, who makes bad choices, who makes choices that bring her more pain. The story of a girl who isn't the archetypal "innocent" victim. She has sex, she drinks, she smokes pot, and she doesn't fully understand that she's allowed to say no. The story of a girl who is judged a lot. And yet her story still counts. And so does mine. And so does yours.

Unfortunately abuse and assault are prolific and common. In our society we don't have a good understanding of consent. If you feel pressured to say yes, that isn't consent. If you say maybe, that isn't consent. If you say I guess, that isn't consent. If you just don't say no, that isn't consent. Maybe you know this theoretically, and maybe it's hard to remember in the moment. Maybe it's hard to stand by your no.

Whether you choose to tell your story or not, it matters.

Thank you for letting me tell my story.

I am so incredibly grateful.

Acknowledgments

This book was written on Ponca land and takes place on Duwamish land. Always remember, we are settlers on stolen land.

Ever Since has had many forms and many friends who have helped me along the way. Thank you to the readers of the earliest version which, believe it or not, was a portal fantasy in which Virginia was a side character. Paula, Mariah, Suzanna, I am so grateful that you suffered through and encouraged me despite my garbagey writing.

Thank you to my writing besties and betas, Arnée, Kelsy, James, Conner, J and Bri, Emma, Suzanna, Noah, Lily, and Ridley. Kinzie, you get a special thank-you for going the extra mile and doing a sensitivity read. And thank you to my other sensitivity reader, Juno. Thank you to the Lovely Winter Sugar Plums (credit to Elnora for the name). I wouldn't have had the courage to do this without you.

Thank you to the agents and editors who provided resources and answered questions, who were helpful and generous with their time, and who gave me kind and encouraging no-thank-yous.

Thank you to Annie, the first industry professional to say

yes to *Ever Since*. You believed in me when I barely believed in myself.

Thank you from the bottom of my heart to my incredible, tremendous, profoundly talented agent, Susan. Thank you for your partnership, your vision, and your championship of Virginia and her story. Thank you to everybody at Upstart Crow.

Thank you to my editor Lauri for everything you've done for me and for this story. Your guidance, skill, and formidable talent have made this process joyful and enlightening. It's not hyperbole to say that working with you has been a dream come true. Thank you to the geniuses over at design, Cerise and Kristie; the careful copyeditors Regina and Kenny; the brilliant marketing and publicity folks Emily, Jordana, Christina, Carmela, Alex, Felicity, Trevor, Venessa, Summer, Shannon, James, and Brianna; the talented sales folks Amanda, Debra, Todd, Enid, Mark, and Cletus; and everyone else at Penguin who worked so lovingly on this project.

An extra thank-you to Susan and Lauri for your support, compassion, and kindness in working with me on such a personal and, at times, difficult project. Every step of the way I have felt safe and cared for. I am so grateful to be a part of this team.

And most of all thank you to my family. My mom, my sister Lily, my nieces Eva and Cat, my children Rowan, Jude, and Sebastian. Your love and support have sustained me in this journey.

And most, most, most of all, thank you to Zack. When we met, and I told you my dream of quitting my job and being a full-time writer, you said okay, let's do this. It took a few years but we did. You gave me my first computer. You read this silly little book about a thousand times, and loved every iteration. You cried with me, you comforted me, you encouraged me, you told me not to quit, you kept me from despair when I thought there was no way I could ever succeed at this impossible dream. But most of all, throughout our entire relationship, you have modeled consent, equal partnership, and compassion. You are the best man I've ever known. I love you forever.

Resources

Sexual violence is a term that can be hard to understand. If you suspect you've been sexually assaulted or abused, here is a useful resource:

www.rainn.org/types-sexual-violence

USA:

www.rainn.org

www.thehotline.org

Global:

nomoredirectory.org

www.unwomen.org/en/what-we-do/ending-violence-against-women/faqs/signs-of-abuse

For trans and nonbinary folks:

www.nsvrc.org/blogs/resources-and-support-transgender-survivors

www.bwss.org/support/lgbtq2s

988 Suicide & Crisis Lifeline:

If you're in crisis and need support, please call or text 988 or go to 988lifeline.org/chat.